Born in Edinburgh in 1906, **John Innes Mackintosh Stewart** was educated at Oriel College, Oxford, where he was presented with the Matthew Arnold Memorial Prize and named a Bishop Frazer's scholar. After graduation he went to Vienna to study Freudian psychoanalysis for a year.

His first book, an edition of Florio's translation of *Montaigne*, got him a lectureship at the University of Leeds. In later years he taught at the universities of Adelaide, Belfast and Oxford.

Under his pseudonym, Michael Innes, he wrote a highly successful series of mystery stories. His most famous character is John Appleby, who inspired a penchant for donnish detective fiction that lasts to this day. His other well-known character is Honeybath, the painter and rather reluctant detective, who first appeared in *The Mysterious Commission*, in 1975.

Stewart's last novel, *Appleby and the Ospreys*, appeared in 1986. He died aged eighty-eight.

D1067164

THE AMPERSAND PAPERS
APPLEBY AND HONEYBATH
APPLEBY AND THE OSPREYS
THE APPLEBY FILE
APPLEBY ON ARARAT
APPLEBY PLAYS CHICKEN
APPLEBY TALKING
APPLEBY TALKS AGAIN
APPLEBY'S ANSWER
APPLEBY'S END
APPLEBY'S OTHER STORY
AN AWKWARD LIE
THE BLOODY WOOD
CARSON'S CONSPIRACY
A CHANGE OF HEIR
CHRISTMAS AT CANDLESHOE
A CONNOISSEUR'S CASE
THE DAFFODIL AFFAIR
DEATH AT THE CHASE
DEATH AT THE PRESIDENT'S LODGING
A FAMILY AFFAIR
FROM LONDON FAR
THE GAY PHOENIX
GOING IT ALONE

HAMLET, REVENGE!
HARE SITTING UP
HONEYBATH'S HAVEN
THE JOURNEYING BOY
LAMENT FOR A MAKER
THE LONG FAREWELL
LORD MULLION'S SECRET
THE MAN FROM THE SEA
MONEY FROM HOLME
THE MYSTERIOUS COMMISSION
THE NEW SONIA WAYWARD
A NIGHT OF ERRORS
OLD HALL, NEW HALL
THE OPEN HOUSE
OPERATION PAX
A PRIVATE VIEW
THE SECRET VANGUARD
SHEIKS AND ADDERS
SILENCE OBSERVED
STOP PRESS
THERE CAME BOTH MIST AND SNOW
THE WEIGHT OF THE EVIDENCE
WHAT HAPPENED AT HAZELWOOD

MICHAEL INNES

APPLEBY AT ALLINGTON

HOUSE OF
STRATUS

This edition published in 2001 by House of Stratus, an imprint of House of Stratus Ltd, Thirsk Industrial Park, York Road, Thirsk, North Yorkshire, YO7 3BX, UK.

www.houseofstratus.com

Typeset, printed and bound by House of Stratus.

A catalogue record for this book is available from the British Library and the Library of Congress.

ISBN 1-84232-713-5

PART ONE

SON ET LUMIÈRE

1

'It's wonderful to have a little peace and quiet for a change,' Owain Allington said. 'And particularly when it takes the form of a congenial *tête-à-tête*.'

Allington was a handsome man in his late fifties. He cultivated – one had to call it that – a slightly old-world air, and every now and then seemed to remember to produce formal courtesies of this sort. But Sir John Appleby, sitting on the other side of the magnificent fireplace in his host's library, thought it unnecessary to utter any articulate response to this particular compliment. It struck him as being rather by way of afterthought. Allington looked tired, and perhaps he was regretting not having decided to pass this first tranquil evening in solitude. But he had invited Appleby to dinner – *en garçon*, since he was a bachelor and since Lady Appleby would not get back from London until next day.

It had been an excellent dinner, for what that was worth. And Owain Allington, whom Appleby scarcely knew, had proved quite an entertaining companion. He did a little too much of the talking, perhaps, but usually remembered to drop in appropriate appeals for comment or judgement. He possessed, too, odd information on a surprising variety of people. The evening had worn away rapidly, and the hour was now late.

'Of course,' Allington was saying, 'I still feel something of a stranger in these parts, even although I have a very tolerable reason for doing nothing of the sort. Certainly I'm still sadly vague about some of my neighbours. Yourself, for instance, my dear Sir John.'

Allington paused on this urbanely formal manner of address. 'I would rather guess that your people have lived round about here for a good many generations?'

'Good Lord, no.' Appleby spoke without impatience, although he realized that Allington had been producing a mere idle pretence of ignorance. 'It's not my part of the world, and I'm not that kind of person. But my wife inherited our present house from an uncle, and we came to live in it when I stopped being a policeman.'

'A policeman? But yes, of course. Scotland Yard. I know all about that.' Allington didn't speak particularly convincingly. 'You must have the devil of a lot of yarns about that sort of thing. Get you to spin some of them one day, I hope. You came up on what might be called the criminal side, I think? Do I express myself oddly? I do look forward to talking a little about it, at some time or other. Criminology's been quite a thing with me. But about country life, and so on. As I was saying, more or less, I'm a new man myself – even if it's in a manner of speaking, eh?'

Appleby, who was finishing a second cigar – and he didn't really care for smoking two cigars – again said nothing. Outside in the soft summer darkness, an owl hooted – a lonely sort of owl, for it had been the first sound for what seemed hours. Allington Park was pitched very much in a rural solitude.

Allington Park. The name spoke at once of the sense in which Owain Allington was *not* a new man. One of his direct forbears, Rupert Allington, had held Allington Castle for King Charles. When Oliver Cromwell had first reduced and then demolished the place – which he did very thoroughly – the ruins and surrounding estate had for some reason passed out of the family. There was, indeed, enough of the castle left to constitute a very respectable picturesque feature in the landscape. It had never been quarried in, one had to suppose, except in the interest of a surreptitiously achieved hovel or pig-sty. And when the Georgian mansion in which Appleby was at present sitting had been built – it had been in the first years of the nineteenth century – a mouldering medieval pile just across one's lake had been very much something to be preserved. Mr Osborne had preserved it.

Mr Osborne had been a successful tallow merchant, very wealthy, and laudably anxious to make his way among the gentry. His name must have helped, since it had been rather a respectable one since Queen Elizabeth's time or thereabout. And Osbornes had been owners of Allington until quite recently. Appleby didn't know why they had parted with the place. There were still some of them round about – living in reduced circumstances of a not very harrowing sort.

As for Owain Allington, he had simply turned up and bought the house and estate – in the romantic manner of Warren Hastings (Judith Appleby ironically said) returning to possess himself of his ancestral Daylesford on the strength of a modest fortune picked up in India. Not that Allington had been a nabob. He was some sort of scientist by calling, and Appleby had a notion he had achieved considerable eminence. But science – or perhaps merely a pertinacious application of the scientific mind to the study of the Stock Exchange – had enriched him in what seemed rather a surprising degree. And here he was – established in his ancestral home and as a small landed proprietor. It was – Appleby reflected uncharitably – the successful Englishman's chosen route to going soft.

'My position in the country, and all that, couldn't be called equivocal, I suppose.' Allington spoke as a man amused, and almost as if divining something of Appleby's thought. 'A walk round the tombs in the parish church will settle that. The Osbornes, you know, had to build themselves a brand new and extremely Gothic-looking vault for the repose of their bones. In the church itself we take up a lot more room than the congregation does. Crusaders, and all the rest of it. Still, I've shoved in, and am a newcomer among all sorts of folk whose great-grandfathers walked at a plough-tail. There's mild entertainment in it.'

'No doubt.' Appleby reflected fleetingly on the weird class-consciousness of his countrymen. 'But I suppose there are duties as well as diversions. The estate must take a certain amount of time, surely. And I gather you're a magistrate, and do a good deal of entertaining, and so forth. Don't you regret the time it takes from your real work? You're a younger man than I am, Allington, by a good way.' Appleby was conscious of slight challenge in his own tone. He hadn't really decided whether he cared for his host or not.

'I've retreated into a backwater, you mean? It may be so – and I confess, my dear fellow, that I do sometimes find myself a little casting about for something to use my brains on.' Allington spoke lightly, and with an effect of increasing amusement. 'But I assure you that even a country gentleman can follow scientific pursuits. And I get a great deal of fun out of quite small projects. Perhaps that's shameful to confess. But there it is. Do you know? It even quite entertained me to take an active part in rigging up all that rot.'

'The *son et lumière*?'

'Yes, but praise the Lord it's over, all the same. I'll never allow it again, my dear Appleby. Everybody was upset by it, one way or another. Even Rasselas – and he's of a reposeful nature.'

Rasselas was a golden Labrador, and he now lay before the small summer fire on a black bearskin rug. He was a well-groomed dog; spun-gold might actually have been his outer integument; one had to suppose that his retrieving days were over, and that he now enjoyed retirement on somewhat the same terms of modest opulence as did his master. And his posture certainly suggested the largest capacity for repose. Contented immobility seemed very much his line. It was hard to believe that Rasselas had really been much disturbed by the entertainment which had lately been going on at Allington.

'For how long did your show run?' Appleby asked.

'Three weeks. It's the shortest time it's economic to set it up for – or at least that's what they put across on me. True enough, probably, since it's a surprisingly elaborate affair. One isn't, of course, bothered with actors and actresses. All that – and a lot of music and battles and bombardments and historical noises in general – comes down canned. It has all been pre-recorded on magnetic tapes, and you make your money simply by playing the blessed things over every night.'

'It's the lighting that's rather a business?'

'Lord, yes. Wires and cables all over the place. But interesting, really. It's into the spectacle that most of the ingenuity goes – and the spectacle simply *is* the lighting. So they've developed no end of tricks. All controlled from one point, too. I'll show you.'

'You got good audiences?'

'Capacity audiences, except on the two nights that it rained. *Chars-à-banc* full of tourists – what they call coaches nowadays. And mostly all fixed up in New York and Chicago. That side of the affair – would you believe it? – took over eighteen months to mount. There are all sorts of vexations you mightn't think about. Insurance, for instance. Wherever all those damned people chose to wander, it seemed I was responsible for any harm that might come to them. Driving their cars into the lake, for instance, or encouraging chunks of the castle to fall on their heads. It cost the moon.'

'I hope it made a profit, all the same?'

'A profit?' There was momentary suspicion in Allington's quick glance. 'Quite a good one, I think. But I didn't do it for the mun. It goes to District Nurses, and Preservation Trusts, and homes for superannuated huntsmen: that sort of thing. I did it because it seemed expected of me. Not a good motive, I expect you'll say. New- man stuff again.'

'I'm very sorry not to have seen it.' Appleby, who deprecated nocturnal entertainments in the open air, remembered that he had let most of the evening pass without producing this civility. 'There must have been no end of historical associations to draw upon.'

'The whole bag of tricks.' Allington produced this humorously but with evident satisfaction. 'Queen Elizabeth slept here, for instance. I went into that rather carefully – and in fact the old girl did. And as for this modern house – well, it seems Winston Churchill once came to lunch in it. Some young Osborne was a pal of his.'

'So the house came in as well as the castle?'

'Now one and now the other – although it was naturally the castle most of the time. They were never both lit up at once. We had the church tower, too, and the twelfth-century dovecot, and this and that in the nearer parts of the park. It wasn't bad value for ten bob. Only

I wish I'd had the wit to cut out the stuff about the treasure. It brought us some damned impertinence straight away, and will probably bring more.' Allington paused. 'Can you,' he asked unexpectedly, 'hear anything now?'

Appleby could certainly hear nothing. Even Rasselas seemed to have the art of slumbering without the slightest suggestion of a wheeze. Outside, the late summer night was extraordinarily still. The countryside was enfolded, one might have said, in a kind of soupy silence.

'Nothing at all,' Appleby said. 'What am I expected to hear?'

'Lord knows. Hoarse whispers, curses, heavy breathing, the thud of sods, the clink of mattocks and spades.' Allington laughed as he offered this comical catalogue. 'It's true enough. You see, I had the script written by a young chap from Oxford, and he was quite sure that buried treasure would go down fearfully well. So there was a passage that was a kind of treasure hunt, with a spot-light prowling here and there in the park, probing into likely places. Coming to rest beneath a mighty oak, for instance, and voices whispering "Is it here, perhaps, that King Charles' treasure lies?" Pretty silly, that one – for who'd try to bury anything sizeable bang under a great tree? Still, the idea seemed harmless, and the audience enjoyed it. But – believe it or not – we've already had people prowling in the small hours with fuddled notions of real treasure-trove. If it goes on, Appleby, I'll set Rasselas to bite great collops out of them.'

'An excellent plan.' Appleby stooped down and stroked Rasselas' ear. Rasselas failed to respond by so much as a twitch. It appeared very doubtful whether he would be much of a performer in the collop-biting line.

'Of course, the local folk wouldn't behave like that. They're my own people, in a sense.' It was quite unaffectedly that Allington produced this feudal reflection. 'Townees from the audience – and I rather suspect some of the technical chaps who set up the show. But at least they clear out tomorrow. I've insisted that the whole affair be dismantled and out of the park by noon. That's because of the fête, you know.'

'I don't know about the fête.'

'You'll think I make a circus of the place every day of the year. But tomorrow's the prescriptive date for our church fête, and I felt they might as well come along and get it over. It's a very modest affair. House and gardens open, a few stalls with old women selling jam, and the vicar running some sort of gambling hell in a tent. My job is to walk around in a grey bowler hat. Have you a grey bowler, Appleby? If so, do come across, and we'll walk around together.'

'I'm afraid I only have a grey topper, which wouldn't be at all the same thing. And I might alarm your vicar, if he knew I was a policeman. But about that treasure, Allington. Do you really suppose there may be anything of the kind buried within or near the castle?'

'Ah!' For a moment Allington hesitated. He was looking at Rasselas attentively, rather as if expecting the creature to raise its head from the rug and offer an opinion. 'Your guess is as good as mine. It's a story told about a good many Cavalier strongholds. And, of course, plenty of people did bury their plate, and so on – if they hadn't melted it down in their unfortunate monarch's cause already. But it seems to stand to reason that what got buried was pretty soon dug up again. I certainly haven't sufficient faith in the story to start hunting round myself.'

2

Appleby felt the topic of buried treasure to have exhausted itself. And the hour was growing very late. He had already made one move to depart, and been restrained by his host. He made a mental note to remember in future that Owain Allington was the type that expects conversation into the small hours.

'It's devilish good of you to keep me company,' Allington said, with his odd effect of divining thought. 'This time tomorrow, I'll have more of it than I require. The fête will be over, but the family's coming down. In time for all the mild fun, I suppose. As a matter of fact, I rather expected an advance-guard this evening.'

'A fairly large house-party?' Appleby asked. He hadn't known that Allington possessed anything that could be called a family.

'Nieces and nephews, you know – nieces and nephews. An elderly bachelor – have you noticed? – is invariably furnished with these. As I say, I thought my nephew Martin Allington might turn up on us after dinner. But he's an unaccountable chap. My heir, I may mention. And don't the others know it.'

'Other nephews?' It didn't seem to Appleby that a man ought to talk about family expectations in this way to a mere acquaintance. But civility required that some question be put.

'As a matter of fact, no. I was speaking loosely. What else I run to is three nieces, two of them married. Faith, Hope, and Charity.'

'They're not really – ?' Appleby checked himself.

'Indeed they are.' Allington laughed a shade maliciously. 'My poor sister-in-law was very devout. It's Faith and Charity who are married – and will be bringing down their kids. Hope's hoping still.'

'I see.' Appleby noticed with satisfaction that his cigar could now be called finished, and he could make a definite move to depart. That had been a cheap sort of joke about Hope. Appleby frowned at Rasselas, still deep within some dream-world of his own. He was reflecting that he seemed to become more, not less, censorious as he grew older. The elderly should be tolerant, surely, and not go about raising their eyebrows at small breaches of taste. He was also reflecting that some name had touched off a fugitive association in his mind. Perhaps it had been Rasselas' name. Why should a distinguished scientist, now grooming himself so wholeheartedly as a country gentleman, give a respectable-looking dog an *outré* name like that? Of course, if one imported a dog from Abyssinia it would be another matter. Perhaps there was something lurkingly freakish about Owain Allington.

But the name that had rung a bell – he suddenly realized – was simply that of Allington's nephew.

'I think I've met Martin Allington,' he said. 'Unless it's another man of the same name.'

'Most interesting,' Allington said. 'How does the one you met make his living?'

'I don't know.'

A moment's silence followed this brief reply. Then, as if some penny had dropped in his mind, Allington made a small, humorous gesture, and laughed softly.

'Of course not,' he said. 'It wouldn't have been before you retired, Appleby, and on one of the fringes of your own concerns? Some other association, no doubt.'

Appleby made no answer. It was true he had retired – but one keeps to the rules, all the same. Leaning forward, he tossed the butt-end of his cigar into the fire.

Every country has its own means of recruiting personnel for its security services. In Great Britain much reliance is placed upon a wide education – width being defined by what one gains in passing rather rapidly through a succession of public schools each a little more tolerant than the last. Of course, not every sort of intrepid individualist will do. Some foibles are frowned on. But the main theory is, no doubt, sound enough. The world's stock of strict moral probity is not high. It is uneconomic to employ it in an area more congenial to those for whom, as a matter of second nature, few holds are barred.

And that – Appleby thought, preparing to take his leave – is why spy stories, unless recklessly romanticized, are necessarily so disagreeable. His own had been quite another world. Still, you cannot have been Chief Commissioner of Metropolitan Police without running into a certain amount of that sort of thing. And that was how he had run into Martin Allington.

'You must tidy this up, Appleby,' the Minister had said. Appleby remembered judging it to have been a surprising command, and not really appropriately addressed to him. But that had been because of the overturned furniture and the pool of blood. No doubt (Appleby told himself now) he had a deplorably literal mind, so that it was a second before he grasped that the Minister was speaking in a metaphorical sense. The real mess was the prospect of publicity, and towards that Appleby's damned dicks (it was thus that the Minister robustly expressed himself) appeared determined to pound their way as fast as their flat feet would carry them.

The damned dicks had included – in addition to several bewildered constables and an ambulance team – two very senior Detective-Inspectors from the CID. These hadn't appreciated being so described at all, and one of them had said roundly to the Minister that when attempted murder, followed by attempted suicide, stared him in the face he hoped he knew where his duty lay. The Minister took this quite well. Although alarmed, he was also rather pleased with himself; that he should himself have come on location, so to speak, immediately an agitated subordinate had brought him the story, showed a vigorous attitude to Departmental detail. The dying man (for Martin Allington was still thought to be that) was a Departmental detail. So, really and truly, would be the whole scandal – whatever it was – if it got into some magistrate's court and so beyond smothering. Smothering was what Sir John Appleby had been got out of bed for. And what tidying up meant was simply hushing up. The Minister made no bones about that. This particular little bit of detail was bloody well going to be buried.

Also present (Appleby recalled) had been a man named Colonel Carruthers. It probably wasn't his real name. He ran the particular side of our national life that had got into trouble that evening. He was in a terrible rage – not so much, it seemed, with young Allington for making a muck of something as with the Minister for butting in. He was accountable only to the PM, he said, and his job would become impossible if any piddling little Cabinet Minister felt entitled to busy around. Appleby had kept out of this piece of protocol. He had quite enough on his hands with the modest demand that he and his officers should compound a felony.

In the spy stories there are favoured persons who hold licences (granted presumably by the Sovereign in Council) to kill anybody who gets too awkwardly in the way. But in real life (if so fantastic a scene of things can be called that) neat dispositions of this sort do not obtain. There is just a vague recognition that incidents do occasionally happen which have to be kept quiet about, and that as a consequence somebody is usually left at risk – whether in point of his own conscience or of the law. This seemed to be Appleby's position – or what the Minister proposed as Appleby's position – now. It had to be coped with. For a start, Appleby tried to collect the facts.

There was nothing to be got from the wounded man. It was true that, when doctored in some way by the police surgeon, he had swum briefly into consciousness. Unfortunately he had devoted this interval to no better purpose than a certain amount of feeble but venomous cursing. In this, the word which it seemed to give him most satisfaction to articulate was 'bitch' – from which it was at least possible to conjecture that there had been a lady in the case. Colonel

Carruthers was not communicative. Allington, he remarked grimly, appeared to have been doing a little on the side, and to have bit off more than he could chew. No doubt there had been a lady, but it looked as if there had been rather a tough gentleman as well.

This was a proposition in which it didn't take Appleby and his assistants long to concur. Whether accompanied by the bitch or not, the tough gentleman had forced his way into Allington's flat. There had been a rough house, including a certain amount of shooting. The intruding force had then departed – perhaps in triumph or perhaps in defeat. Allington had then tried to shoot himself, and had made rather a mess of the job. He had been in a panic, one had to suppose.

At this point the police surgeon had announced, with no particular satisfaction, that the wounded man was going to survive, after all. It was a simplification, and a further simplification followed. Allington appeared to have fired three shots – the last of them being into his own person. Appleby started a hunt for the other two bullets. They were found almost at once, embedded rather high up in one of the walls of the room. It was extremely improbable that they could have done any mischief on their way there, so one didn't have to worry about the possibility of another wounded man somewhere around London in consequence of this fracas. As a Secret Agent (if that was the formal way to describe him) Martin Allington appeared to be a singularly poor buy.

And the affair had ended there – shockingly in hugger-mugger, as such things may do. Nobody was brought before a magistrate, and the security of the realm was no doubt vastly fortified as a result. Appleby was not at all pleased with having had anything to do with it, and no further information ever came to him. It seemed natural to suppose that it had ended with young Allington out of a job. He had mixed up his professional affairs – it was the only possible interpretation – with some shady project of his own; had made a mess of this; and had been so convinced that the consequences were going to be disastrous to him that he had shot himself in a blind funk. The probability was that he deserved to be in gaol at this moment. Yet he might simply have ended up with promotion. At this very moment, he might positively be Colonel Carruthers' white-headed boy. The Carruthers world was quite as crazy as that.

And Appleby's chief memory of the business was an uncomfortable one, which he would have wished to forget. He had disliked Martin Allington. Martin Allington had been merely a supine figure under a grey blanket, a blanched and bloodied face, a racked figure fighting for life. Appleby had been repelled by him, nevertheless. It was a nasty thought.

'Martin is a delightful chap.' It was with a start that Appleby recovered from his retrospection on hearing these words. Owain Allington was again looking expectantly at Rasselas, rather as if he wanted the sagacious creature to offer some remark supporting this solid family line. 'And I'm sure he will enjoy meeting you again.'

'I think I may have misled you,' Appleby said. 'I've met your nephew, after a fashion, but I'm not sure he can be said to have met me. He had – well, passed out.'

'Dear me!' If Allington was startled by this odd remark he didn't show it. 'Martin does drink a little too much at times, no doubt. And that reminds me –' He broke off – perhaps because Appleby had shown signs of getting to his feet, or perhaps because Rasselas had actually done so. Rasselas must suddenly have decided it was time to speed the parting guest, for he was no sooner on his paws than he gave Appleby a challenging glance and moved rapidly to the door of the library. 'I can see we have whisky,' Allington went on, 'but I'm sure you like ice.' He leant forward and pressed an electric bell. 'It's something Enzo regularly forgets. Italians are pleasant enough in their way, but far from being as reliable as English servants in the old style.'

'I'm quite sure I don't want ice.' Appleby, now unchallengeably on his feet, glanced towards a side-table. 'But a very little whisky, and a splash of soda, will be just right. I'm afraid it's shockingly late, and I hope you won't blame Enzo if he's already in bed.' Allington, Appleby was reflecting, was rather more fussy about services than a man of presumably intellectual habit ought to be. 'And Rasselas is ready for bed as well.'

'He's proposing to see you to your car.' Allington poured whisky, and the two men drank. 'You must be right about that lad who was supposed to wait up,' Allington said, after some minutes passed. 'He's gone to bed. But I don't expect it's beyond me to find you your coat.'

'I haven't brought a coat,' Appleby put down his glass. 'Thank you for a very pleasant evening.'

They left the house together and walked down a long terrace. Rasselas vanished into the soft darkness. The night was rather warm and completely still.

'If we go down these steps,' Allington said, 'we'll find your car just round a corner.' He flashed a torch which he had picked up in the hall. 'Can you see? The auditorium, as I suppose it should be called, is straight ahead. And over to the left is the control point for the whole show. I wonder whether the juice is still on? I could give you a private performance.'

Appleby didn't want a private performance; he wanted only to get home and go to sleep. But Owain Allington's hospitable zeal had unfortunately renewed itself, and there was nothing to do except follow him across a broad expanse of turf. Presently what appeared to be an improbably vast wall rose up before them in uncertain silhouette against a sky dimly powdered with stars. It was tier upon tier of seats raised over scaffolding.

'The house and the castle,' Allington said, 'and the end of the lake in between. You get all that from anywhere up there. But you get it from this affair too. Naturally, the chap who twiddles the knobs has to have his eye on the whole thing. Do you mind the short ladder? It's quite safe.'

Appleby didn't mind a short ladder, and he put on a decent show of climbing with alacrity. There was a strain of naivety, he had decided, in this eminent retired scientist. Allington was as proud of his *son et lumière* as a small boy with a new model railway. And he was determined to show it off before letting his guest go.

'You might call it a gazebo,' Allington's voice said from up above. He had climbed first. 'Hold hard, and I'll see if the electricity's really on. No go if it isn't. Ah!'

There had been a faint click. Appleby emerged into a glass-sided chamber now faintly visible in a low amber light.

'It might be the cockpit of an air-liner,' Allington said. 'Or the place from which they conduct the business of a battleship. Almost frightening, in a way. All in the interest of a ninety-minute *divertissement.* We live in a very artificial age.'

3

It was a surprisingly roomy place to be perched in air as it was, and in addition to the elaborate equipment for projecting the spectacle there seemed to be much miscellaneous lumber flung into corners and stuffed under benches. In the dim light Appleby could also just distinguish a small table with punctured beer cans, crumpled sandwich papers and empty cigarette cartons.

'They seem to have made it a home from home,' he said.

'They certainly do. I had them put up in the local pub, which is said to be thoroughly comfortable. But they camped here most of the time. Rather a long-haired crowd, and I can't say that I took to them. The top man gave himself artist's airs in a big way. He might have been taking time off from producing grand opera at Covent Garden.' Owain Allington laughed contemptuously in the near-darkness. 'But he knew his stuff, all the same. Handled all these dials and switches in a genuinely sensitive and loving way. He reminded me of a cathedral organist, as a matter of fact. And – do you know? – the show improved night by night.' Allington's pride in the *son et lumière* was again peeping through. 'As it was all prefabricated and sent down from London in boxes, you'd hardly suppose that to be possible. But, of course, there's a certain scope for nuance in fading the different bits and pieces in and out. Have a go.'

'Take a stab at all this stuff?' Appleby was amused. 'I hardly think so. The most dreadful things might happen.'

'I can promise you nothing will blow up.' Allington spoke lightly. He sounded rather offended, all the same. It was as if he had offered a treat to a small boy – to hold the wheel, to perch on the saddle – and had it turned down. Appleby felt that, at least for a minute or two, he must accept this absurd role. And Allington, who had been investigating, spoke again. 'I'm afraid the sound is off. They've taken out the tapes.' He was clearly disappointed. 'But the lighting's in order.'

Appleby looked through the sheet of glass in front of him. To his left he could just distinguish the house, which was in darkness except for half a dozen outdoor lamps which he knew followed the curve of the terrace.

'The switches are simple on-and-off affairs,' Allington said encouragingly. 'The knobs with the calibrations are rheostats. Did you ever hear of composing symphonies out of colours instead of musical notes? There was some aesthetic character who had the notion of it years ago. But he hadn't the technical know-how. It could be done now, with a contraption rather like this. Let's have at least a sonata, Appleby.'

Appleby put out a hand and flicked a switch – a shade impatiently, since he was beginning to think all this pretty silly. All that happened was that the arc of lights on the terrace vanished.

'Try again, my dear fellow.' This effect of defeated expectation appeared to have amused Allington very much, for he was laughing loudly. 'We'll call that the tap of the conductor's baton, calling the orchestra to order. And over the audience a hush descends. Now carry on.'

'All right – and we'll begin by having those back again.' Appleby flicked the same switch, and the lights on the terrace reappeared. 'Now we'll try the one next door… How very odd!' This time, instead of vanishing, the sickle of lights had played a sort of leapfrog over the arm of the lake which separated the house from the castle, so that they now appeared far to Appleby's right.

'Interesting,' Allington said, ' – although not one of the designed effects. Shove in that button just above.'

Appleby shoved in the button, and at once the lights changed colour and form. They were now flickering and ruddy.

'That's it!' Allington was delighted. 'Torches, you know. A curved line of torches in front of the castle when there was a grand outdoor masque to amuse Queen Elizabeth. There was a complete sea-battle on the lake, culminating in the appearance of Neptune and a lot of tritons. Neptune made a speech in praise of Her Highness and in celebration of English valour. In 1589, that is. In 1967 we didn't manage the ships or the mythology. But we had the gunfire, and the voices of both Neptune and the Queen. It was a great success.'

'I'm sure it was.' Appleby manipulated another switch. This time, the effect was spectacular. The whole castle had appeared in a blaze of light. 'Well, I'm blessed!' Appleby said. 'Castle Dargan's ruins all lit.'

'What's that?'

'Just some poem by Yeats. The Electricity Board, by the way, must have had quite a business bringing you all that juice.'

'They're going to send in the devil of a bill. Try the one to the left.'

The one to the left set the castle on fire – or presented a very colourable appearance of that. The flames leapt and flared in the night. The Roundheads, it was to be presumed, were burning the place down. Appleby flicked the switch again. The fatal conflagration instantly vanished.

'It's all most ingenious,' he said. He was now dreadfully sleepy, and indisposed entirely to conceal the fact. 'But I'm not sure there isn't more fun in fireworks.'

Allington accepted this hint of satiety, and made a movement to depart.

'I think I'm a bit of a showman,' he said. 'So I get rather fascinated by this sort of thing. Still, I've had enough of it. So let's go. Unless, of course, you'd like me to turn on the part about the treasure.'

'It might set me digging in your park in the small hours. So I think I'd better call it a day.' Appleby moved towards the trapdoor guarding the ladder. 'It seems to me, by the way, that they'll be pretty smart if they get this whole installation away by noon tomorrow.' He glanced at his watch. 'I ought to say by noon today.'

'I rather agree – although I've told them they must be at work at first light.' Allington took a final glance around. 'There's an uncommon lot of junk even up here. What's that bundle of stuff in the corner?'

Appleby followed Allington's glance. Gazing out, as they had been doing, at a succession of illuminations, they still saw little by the low amber light in which they stood.

'Surely – ' Appleby said, and broke off. He reached the corner in three strides, stooped down and suddenly went very still. It was the better part of a minute before he straightened up again. 'It's not a bundle of stuff,' he said. 'It's a man.'

'It's *what*?' Allington spoke on a note of mingled bewilderment and sharp alarm.

'It's a man,' Appleby repeated grimly. 'And I think he's dead.'

However it may have been with Owain Allington, Appleby had seen too many dead men in unexpected places and mysterious circumstances to be particularly staggered upon the present occasion. He even detected himself as reflecting that, had he been sufficiently strong-minded to decline this poking around the scene of the *son et lumière*, he would not have got himself thus tiresomely involved with whatever unfortunate thing had happened.

He also found time to be thankful – and rather brutally to tell Allington that he should be similarly thankful – that he wasn't dead himself. For what had taken place was presently fairly clear. This ridiculous elevated box, with its mass of electrical equipment, had been casually left by the persons responsible for it in a highly dangerous state. Or – for it would be necessary to be very fair in the matter – in a state that was decidedly far from fool-proof. And this chap had climbed in and got himself electrocuted.

It could hardly be anybody's excuse that he was trespassing, and that nothing of the kind was to have been expected. The *son et lumière* at Allington Park must have been the talk of a dozen surrounding villages, and curiosity about this structure was as natural as if it had been a tripod arrived from Mars. Appleby's brow darkened as he reflected that half a dozen venturesome children might have gone scrambling up that ladder in the dark.

Allington had found a master-switch, and the place was now safe enough. But, for the moment, this seemed to represent the limit of his nervous resources. He was badly shaken – which wasn't, Appleby reflected, surprising in the least. Here were the two of them, in darkness except for an unimpressive electric torch, perched at the top of a ladder with a totally unexplained and unexpected corpse.

'A tramp,' Allington said. 'He must have decided to find shelter here for the night.'

'Perhaps so.' Appleby made a further, and necessarily imperfect, examination of the dead man. He looked about twenty-five, and he had ginger hair. He certainly bore no appearance of belonging to the higher classes of society. 'It's a pity that even the lights on your terrace are out. I suppose they're the only part of the electrical equipment over there still to be tied up with all this?'

'Oh, certainly. I had most of that part of the damned nonsense cleared up this morning.' Allington no longer seemed particularly proud of his *son et lumière.*

'It can't be helped. You'd better get back to the house, and leave me here. Take your torch. Call the police. And call your own doctor, as well. He won't thank you, but he'll no doubt turn out promptly for the squire. When this sort of thing happens, it's sometimes useful to have an additional observer around. And it might be useful with the insurance people.'

'The insurance people?'

'Certainly. You were talking about them. Whoever this chap is, and however unauthorized his entry here, anybody who depended upon him would have a bit of a case against someone.' Appleby spoke dryly. 'It may sound callous, but one has to have a thought to these small practical matters. And rouse your servants, and have them bring over rugs and hot-water bottles as quick as they can.'

'But surely – '

'The man's dead, all right, but we're not doctors. It's prudent to take every practical measure. You'll sound less of a fool at the inquest.' Appleby checked this note of irritation, since it was something not very decent to express. 'I'm afraid you're a bit shaken, Allington, and

I'm sorry to sound brusque. But the sooner we have the proper measures under way – well, the sooner we can relax a little.'

'I'll go at once.' But Allington was still irresolute. 'I wish Martin really had turned up this evening. I rather expected him, as I think I told you. He'd be a support.'

'You're going to have plenty of support tomorrow – and a church fête as well. Meanwhile, I'll do what I can myself.'

'My dear chap, you're very kind. And I'm sorry that the place has produced so shocking an end to your dining with me. I feel it almost as a breach of hospitality.'

Judging this proposition to be decidedly overstrained, Appleby made no reply to it. He watched Owain Allington climb down the ladder and begin to cross the strip of park in front of the invisible house. Then he turned back to keep his vigil by the dead man. The *son et lumière* at Allington had certainly had an unfortunate close. But in about half an hour, he told himself, it would cease to be his affair. No doubt he would be required to give evidence before the coroner. But that, after all, was something he had done before.

Meanwhile, inactivity was his role. He had satisfied himself that the man in the corner was dead, and further than that he had better not go. There must be an investigation, no doubt, although there didn't really seem to be all that to investigate. But it wasn't for a retired Police Commissioner to start poking around. If he did so, the local people would be entirely respectful. They would feel mildly outraged, all the same.

But inactivity wasn't natural to him. He moved over to one of the glass panels shutting him off from the night, and found that it was designed to slide back in a groove. There would be no harm in letting in a little more air. He did so, and was presently leaning out into the darkness. Being thus less immediately in the presence of death, he decided it wouldn't be too strikingly improper to light a cigarette. For a moment the brief flare of the match blinded him. Then he realized that the summer night into which he was gazing was no longer all but impenetrably dark. For a moment he thought that the dawn was breaking, and then he saw that he was witnessing one of those odd meteorological occasions, disconcerting to nocturnally-behaving persons, in which the moon heaves itself into the sky not all that far ahead of the sun. It was a very faint moonlight that was seeping with a slow stealth into the park.

It was with a sense that time had been behaving in some obscurely curious fashion that night that he now glanced at the illuminated dial of his watch. There would certainly be little of the night left by the time he got to bed. Meanwhile, there was this mild lunar manifestation. It would be soothing, even perhaps poetic in suggestion to anyone less gruesomely circumstanced than he himself happened to be. Even so, he watched with satisfaction great trees beginning to define themselves – beginning even, or so he fancied, to cast a ghost of shadow on the grass. He remembered the story about King Charles' treasure being buried under one of them. He was very far from believing in it, and it was his impression that Owain Allington was very far from believing in it too. But there had apparently been people taking it seriously – even to the point of doing a little quiet trespassing and prospecting at an hour very much like this. It suddenly occurred to Appleby that the dead man might have been one of them.

He turned back irresolutely towards the body, almost as if prompted to seek verification of this suspicion in some way. But that was nonsense, like a notion out of a boys' adventure story – in which the dead man would prove to have an ancient map in his pocket, with the hiding-place marked with a cross in rusty red.

Appleby returned to the window. He could now see the glimmer of the lake, and even the white line of the long drive that skirted it. Low on a near horizon, a beam of light appeared, circled, vanished. That was a car or lorry on the high road. Presently the arrival of the county constabulary would be signalised in that way. And he himself would drive home in the first dawn – drive home without having interfered.

Of course, one can't help one's thoughts. Appleby found himself at least thinking about the dead man. How long had he been dead? He remembered the first feel of the body under his hand. He and Allington – he had told Allington – were not doctors. But there are some things one develops an instinct for if one has become Police Commissioner by the long, hard road of half a lifetime of criminal investigation.

No time at all, Appleby had to tell himself. The fellow had been dead no time at all.

4

'It sounds very odd to me,' Judith Appleby said.

'It was no business of mine,' her husband replied. 'I must get that bird out.' A thrush had got under the net guarding the raspberries, and for a couple of minutes he devoted himself to ejecting it. 'I'm not a policeman,' he then said. 'Or not any longer.'

'John, dear, whenever you meet anybody you judge to be a socially pretentious person, the first thing you announce is that you *are* a policeman. It's like some City gent in a Victorian novel, bellowing that he's a plain British merchant.'

'All right, all right. But stick to the point. This rum death at Allington is *not* my concern. And there's another of those confounded birds. These nets are no good. They're a notion out of Noah's Ark. This winter we'll have Hoobin and his boy build cages. We'll put all the soft fruit inside cages. It's the only way. I've been thinking about it for some time.'

'Cages, by all means.' Judith clapped her hands expertly behind the second thrush. She had come home by the mid-morning train, and they were making a round of the garden. 'And perhaps you should keep bees. There's said to be a lot of intellectual interest in them. You could embody your observations and researches in what used to be called a monograph.' She lowered the net into place again. 'Of course, I can see that this affair is very old-hat.'

'What do you mean – old-hat?'

'*Death at Allington Park*. It sounds like the most antique sort of detective story. But, in fact, it's something that has happened to one of our neighbours. And it's unexplained.'

'It doesn't seem to be a neighbour who got himself killed. The body conveyed nothing to Owain Allington. As for its being unexplained – it's early days to say that. No doubt the police and the medical people will work it out.'

'I suppose, John, you'll have to answer questions yourself?'

'No doubt.'

'Do you know, I doubt whether you're going to strike your local colleagues as a man of much observation. How large is this gazebo-thing the show was run from?'

'Surprisingly large to be perched up on stilts like that. Perhaps twelve feet square – if my observation *is* any good, that is.' Appleby looked dubiously at Judith. What she was going to say wasn't exactly obscure to him.

'And you were shut up in it for quite some time, fooling around with that *lumière*, and quite unconscious that you were cheek by jowl with a corpse?'

'There was only a very low light. And no question of being cheek by jowl with the thing. It was crumpled in a corner, and more or less under a bench.'

'That's one of the things which don't make sense. The electrocuting was of the instantaneous sort, and not the nasty hang-on-until-charred business?'

'It was nasty enough. But you're quite right.'

'Otherwise, there would have been a kind of cook-house smell.' Judith made this revolting point dispassionately. 'So I don't see how – '

'No more do I. It was curious that the chap tumbled himself so unobtrusively into a corner.'

'It was Owain Allington who went up the ladder first?'

'Yes.'

'Into the dark?'

'Yes.' Appleby smiled at his wife. 'We're quite getting somewhere, are we not?'

'The first thing Allington did was to shove the corpse out of the way. Then he switched on this low light as Sir John Appleby – a dignified figure who is not to be hurried – lumbered majestically up the ladder.'

'Laughter in court,' Appleby said. 'The witness appeared discomfited.'

'But it still doesn't make sense. For why should he do anything of the sort?'

'Why, indeed?' Appleby looked worried – but this was because he had failed to count accurately the peaches on the old brick wall which they were now facing. 'Perhaps I haven't made it clear that my lack of observation continued to the end. I'd have left the blessed gazebo as ignorant of the corpse as I'd entered it, if Allington himself hadn't absolutely invited me to find it.'

'You mean that he said, "Look, Appleby, there's a dead body"?'

'Not precisely that. He said, "What's that bundle of stuff in the corner?" And I went over and found what I found. If he knew the body was there – and it's a perfectly fantastic notion, anyway – and wanted me to find it, he might as well have let me find it at the start, and not made a dive for it when he first entered the place, in order to shove it out of sight for a time. Isn't that obvious?'

'Not in the least. He may have felt that an extra ten or fifteen minutes would make it more certain that the chap really was dead.'

'You have the most macabre imagination of any woman I have ever known. Here is some wretched accident with a live electric cable, and you start fumbling round to find something suspicious in the behaviour of a highly respectable landed proprietor.'

'You oughtn't to expect *me* to do any more than fumble. I'm just an amateur. But you're a professional, and ought to be able to get straight at the truth.' Judith produced this argument with a great air of lucidity. 'It would be dreadful if poor Mr Allington *did* come under any sort of suspicion. So I think you owe it to – '

'Considering that you've just been cooking up a sheer rigmarole against the fellow – ' Words failed Appleby. 'I think I'll spray this one,' he said. 'I don't like the look of the leaves. I'll do it this afternoon.'

'But, John, we'll be at the fête.'

'Fête! What fête?' Appleby looked at his wife in alarm. 'I detest fêtes.'

'The fête at Allington, of course.' Judith seemed entirely surprised.

'There can't be a fête at Allington. A death yesterday, and a fête worse than death today: it just wouldn't do.' Appleby paused, but this fatigued joke raised no mirth in Judith. 'They're bound to put it off.'

'I don't think so.' Judith shook her head decisively. 'Not just for an unfortunate accident.'

'You've just been maintaining –'

'It will give you another chance to look around.'

'I don't want another chance to look around. I refuse to go to Allington's wretched fête. The vicar over there runs a gambling hell. It's something that, in my position, I ought not to countenance.'

'I really think you must, John. It wouldn't be civil to Wilfred Osborne not to.'

'Wilfred Osborne? What the dickens has he got to do with it?'

'He makes a point of always going to the affair at the Park. As the former owner, he feels it would be ungracious to stay away.'

'Very proper, no doubt. But I don't see what it has to do with us.'

'John, it's why I came back by the early train. I've asked Wilfred to lunch, and said we'll all go across together.' Judith glanced across the garden. 'And here he is.'

Osborne, spare and oddly elegant in ancient tweeds, gave them a wave – genial, but at the same time indicating that Sir John and Lady Appleby must wait their turn. Osborne was conversing with their gardener, the aged Hoobin. The exchange began with formal courtesies, modulated into lively and contentious debate, and closed upon what appeared to be a note of harmonious despondency. Hoobin shook his head gloomily at Mr Osborne, and Mr Osborne shook his head gloomily at Hoobin. The fatality that lies in wait for all horticultural endeavour was common ground between them.

'Judith, my dear, you look extremely well.' Osborne kissed his hostess and shook hands with Appleby. 'How are you, Appleby? Not too bored, eh? Very little scope for the fingerprints, and all that, in Long Dream, I should say.'

Appleby made a suitable reply to this humorous sally. He had done a great deal of living on terms of mild acquaintanceship with people who appeared to have known his wife intimately from her cradle. He rather liked Wilfred Osborne. His conversation could scarcely be called intellectually stimulating, but it was inoffensive even when slightly absurd. And his manners were of the kind that can't go wrong; he had the flawless confidence and the polite diffidence of a man who has never had to give his position in the world a thought. It was a position which had, indeed, taken quite a tumble. Like Dogberry, Osborne must have had losses, since he had once lived in a large way and now lived in a small one. But there was not the slightest sign that this change in material circumstances had made any mark upon him. He was today what from his birth he had been. The great-grandson of the tallow King of Victoria's middle time seemed to embody the aristocratic idea much more securely than did the descendant of the Cavaliers and Crusaders who had supplanted him at Allington Park.

'Hoobin is worried about the moles,' Osborne said. 'And quite right, too. Your upper spinney's alive with them, and it stands to reason they have to get down to the stream. And you can see what that means, Judith. It means your croquet lawn. One day you'll ask all your friends to a tournament – all those dead-keen old ladies and gentlemen, my dear – and they'll all spend a wakeful night planning the what-d'you-call-it – the strategy of their game. But that same night the moles will have been at work. So when the company arrives, brandishing its mallets – '

'It sounds a catastrophe,' Appleby said. 'So what should we do?'

'You'll find that Hoobin wants to bring in the mole-catcher. But that's because he has a family interest. It's Hannah Hoobin's boy who is our local mole-catcher now.'

'*Hannah* Hoobin's boy?' Appleby was now accustomed to this sort of conversation. 'Is that the old fellow with the grey beard?'

'That's Hannah Hoobin's boy. But have nothing to do with him, Appleby. Shoot the creatures. It's the only way.'

'Shoot them!' Appleby was dismayed. 'I shoot squirrels, and I shoot pigeons, and I rather think that soon I shall have to be shooting rabbits. But I'm blest if I'm going to start on the moles. Besides, I don't think I've ever actually seen a live mole in my life. They're of a reclusive habit, I'd say.'

'My dear Appleby, you don't need to *see* them.' Osborne was harmlessly amused by this innocence. 'You get a stepladder, set it up over each mole-hill in turn, and fire straight down into it. Of course the timing's important. Moles, you know, go by the clock. Twelve noon used to be the time. But that was in the old days. Summer time may make it a bit chancy. In which case, I'd try moth-balls. Moles don't care for moth-balls at all.'

'I think, perhaps, we should go in and begin lunch,' Judith said. She felt that John might support all this rural lore better over his cold salmon and hock. 'And we don't want to miss the opening of the fête. That's always fun.'

'Judith and I missed the *son et lumière*,' Appleby said over the coffee. 'But Allington gave me an account of it last night. He appears to have enjoyed it, really – although he was putting on a bit of a turn about how upsetting it had been.'

'And now,' Judith said, 'there really *has* been an upset. Have you heard, Wilfred? Mr Allington took John to look at the lighting equipment last night, and they found a dead man. He had received a lethal electric shock.'

'Good Lord!' Osborne had put down his cup. He looked very startled. 'Somebody who had strayed in?'

'He was still unidentified when I came away,' Appleby said. 'It does look as if it may have been a matter of rash curiosity. And Allington has a curious story about one consequence of this show he has been putting on. There was something about treasure in it – and people have actually been found wandering about the park in the night, treasure-hunting. It sounded a bit unlikely to me, and I couldn't be certain that Allington himself was being quite serious about it.'

'There was always a legend about treasure.' Osborne spoke thoughtfully. 'I remember it quite firing my imagination as a boy. In fact, my brother and I went digging for it. I haven't thought about it for years, but no doubt the story still lives on. It's rather a pleasant memory, so far as I'm concerned. I'd hate to think of it leading to anybody's death.'

'No need to, at the moment.' Appleby gave a brief account of his experience of the previous night. 'I can't see how any notion of hunting for treasure would take a chap up among all that electrical stuff.' Appleby paused, suddenly frowning. 'Osborne, you attended this affair?'

'I went along on the first night. As Judith knows, I'm careful not to seem standoffish about anything at Allington. And this was a good idea, without a doubt. Jolly well done, I thought, and pots of money for charity.'

'Did the part about the treasure suggest one likely spot for it more than another?'

'I don't very clearly remember. To tell you the honest truth, Appleby, I got a bit sleepy at times. History, and all that, tends to have that effect on me, I'm afraid. Not that it wasn't tiptop, as I said. There was what you might call a will-o'-the-wisp effect when they told about the treasure. You know what I mean: lights darting here and there, and always deeper into the park. Come to think of it, they always seemed to end up in the same spot. As if that was the goal, you know. But it was very confusing. That was the idea, I suppose. The place wouldn't have been easy to identify afterwards.' Osborne shook his head. 'I see what you're getting at, of course. But it would only be a wholly uneducated person – indeed, a half-wit, wouldn't you say? – who could take anything of the sort as other than make-believe. No sensible person could suppose that an *actual* likely hiding-place was being – what's it called? – spot-lit.'

'That seems fair enough.' Appleby saw that Judith was looking at her watch; she seemed genuinely determined to be at Allington in time for the start of the afternoon's proceedings. 'But suppose it *was* rational to believe that the will-o'-the-wisp was a reliable guide. There might then be sense in turning it on again, in order to take accurate observations at leisure. Allington actually invited me to get going on it myself. I don't at all know how it would have been done, since all I ever did last night was to flick a switch or two at random. But one imagines there must have been some sort of script or score or notation. The whole affair – the *lumière* part, I mean – must have been programmed to go through certain sequences at command. You'd do this or that, and the treasure-hunt sequence would result – duly synchronized, of course, with the relevant chunks of *son.* It is just conceivable – and I may say, Osborne, that it's Judith who has set me taking such a fantastic view of the affair – it is just conceivable that the chap who came to that nasty end thought that, there under his hand, he had some clue to finding the treasure.' Appleby paused. 'I don't think it likely. But it's a line. It's *one* line – for a start.'

'I'll get out the car,' Judith said and slipped quietly from the room.

'Osborne,' Appleby asked thoughtfully, 'I think you did know Judith from her earliest years?'

'Certainly. I can remember her in bonnets and long clothes. Queer things they dressed infants in in those days.'

'Would you say that, from the first, she was peculiarly adept at getting her own way?'

'That puts it a little strongly, perhaps.' Wilfred Osborne wasn't at all at a loss before this question. 'But she had marked strength of character from the first. Most important in the – what would you call it? – battle of life. I often reflected that the fellow who married her would bless himself. Splendid housewife, too – eh? Capital lunch.'

33

5

It appeared that the annual fête at Allington Park was not quite so modest and local an affair as Owain Allington had intimated. People came from both the Dreams (Stony Dream and the Applebys' own Long Dream), from Linger, and even from Boxer's Bottom. None of them had any direct interest in the objects of this particular charitable effort. In the village hall of Allington all the doors had come off their hinges and half the windows had fallen out of their frames – but who at Linger cared about that? In inclement weather rainwater dripped down the neck of the Reverend Mr Scrape as he murmured from his pulpit to Owain Allington, Owain Allington's farm-manager, Owain Allington's farm-manager's wife, old Scurl (who rang the bell), and the assembled young of Allington village, penned mute in the chancel, and facetiously referred to as the choir. Yet this would hardly have struck anybody in Boxer's Bottom as anything out of the way. The grand project for a changing-room and lavatory on the new playing-field (gift of Owain Allington Esquire), if bruited in any of these other rural centres, would doubtless have been commented upon as a mere delusion of grandeur.

Nevertheless, people poured into Allington Park. The men came to shoot clay pigeons under the superintendence of Owain Allington's keeper, and also in the hope that one or another of their children would win not a lollipop or a comic but a bottle of whisky or gin from the threepenny lottery. The children came to ride the ponies of their more fortunately circumstanced contemporaries, to scream, to run, to collide with each other and with the adults, and occasionally to fall into the lake. The women came to gossip – and in the perennial hope that the gentry, whether in miserable ignorance or to curry favour, would be selling their fruitcakes and chutney and jam well below market prices. These may be declared the main motivating forces at play within this wholesome English festival.

It was a beautiful afternoon, and the sunlight glittered on the lake as Appleby swung the car into the long drive that led straight up to the north front of the house. The castle was visible across the water and slightly to the west; what wasn't visible was the scaffolding erected for the *son et lumière*. Sure enough, it had vanished, and in its place was a marquee and some smaller tents. A faint waft of music came across the lake. Owain Allington's flag was flying from his housetop.

'Quick work,' Appleby said. And then, suddenly, he exclaimed. 'Do you know? I think they've taken away the gazebo-affair too.'

'It would have been rather a skeleton at the feast, eh?' Osborne suggested. 'At a junketing like this you don't want a standing reminder – quite literally standing, one may say – of a rather gruesome happening the day before.'

'True enough. But I'm surprised at the police. When you have an unexplained fatality in a temporary structure like that, you don't generally whisk it out of existence twelve hours later.'

'Owain would have insisted on it.' Osborne spoke innocently if a shade dryly. 'It's wonderful what can be insisted on by a grandee – wouldn't you say?'

'Particularly in the green heart of England,' Judith amplified. She had marked her husband's disapproval, and regarded it as highly promising. 'Perhaps, John, you'll be able to have a little chat about it with Colonel Pride.'

'The Chief Constable? Certainly not. He feels I have to be kept in my place – which is absurd. If he's at this nonsense, of course we'll have some civil talk. But I don't care for him.'

'My dear Appleby, you mustn't be put out by Tommy Pride's manner.' Wilfred Osborne spoke as a man of peace. 'He's not a bad chap. Had quite a decent war, and all that. Perhaps he hasn't much between the ears, as the young people say. And, naturally, he knows nothing about criminals, and all that sort of thing.' Osborne paused in mild perplexity before Judith's sudden yelp of laughter. 'Only saying, my dear, that poor old Tommy may feel a bit defensive – with a top pro. like John moving into these parts. Appleby, may I call you John? Seems not too out of turn.'

'Yes, of course. And I've no doubt you're right, Wilfred, about Pride. But he's one reason why I wouldn't dream of starting to poke into that affair last night.'

'Why do the lake and drive run beside each other on this hard straight line?' Judith had judged a diversion useful. 'Didn't Humphrey Repton or somebody lay out the grounds?'

'He improved them, my dear. That was the word.' Osborne was delighted. 'It comes into *An Inquiry into the Changes of Taste in Landscape Gardening.* And it was only for my great-grandfather, you know, that he did the job. Chronologically, that's rather remarkable. Osbornes marry late, you see, if they marry at all. My great-grandfather was what they called a Russia merchant. I don't know why Russia. It was where tallow in a big way seemed to come from. Perhaps it was made out of bears. What was I saying?'

'Repton.'

'Yes, of course. He was a gentleman, you know, who lost his fortune and turned professional gardener to the nobility, gentry, and newer propertied classes. That would be how to put it – eh, John? And it impressed my great-grandfather very much. He had Repton in a big way. In those days you *wound* your waters – that was the word for them – but just here it was necessary to have this long straight bank. It's really the bed of a shallow quarry, from which they got the stone for the later parts of the castle. However, the resourceful Repton said it was an interesting return to the Dutch Taste. I believe he threw in a tulip-bed a quarter of a mile long. Of course, this isn't the main approach. Do you know Ashdown House in Berkshire? Most intriguing Dutch place in the country.'

The car continued to move up the drive – slowly, because it was now one of a line of cars. Osborne continued to talk in a casually informative way about Allington. Appleby wondered how strong his feelings about the house really were. He also wondered whether, apart from having been a soldier, this amiable elderly man had ever engaged in any settled occupation whatever. Presumably he had run Allington when he owned it. But what had he done since then? Perhaps just lived on what he had salved from what must have been, presumably, a sadly encumbered estate. Judith would know.

The music had sounded quite grand from far away, as if it were provided by a regimental band. It turned out, however, to utter itself from a van, the property of young William Goodcoal, who owned the wireless shop in Linger. The van was boldly lettered PUBLIC ADDRESS SYSTEM, and justified this claim by every now and then breaking away from melody into a curious dry crackling, susceptible of uncertain interpretation as a human voice commending to the general regard any of the surrounding attractions being inadequately patronized at the moment. There was another van vending ice-cream – conceivably in the interest of new doors and windows for the village hall, but more probably in a spirit of successful piracy and private enterprise. Between two splendid oaks in a nearer reach of the park a long trestle table had been set up, and behind this the females of middling station in Allington and round about were preparing to dispense teas at half-a-crown a time. Nearby, a commodious bathing-tent, decorated with sphinx's heads, crescent moons, broomsticks and similar objects suggestive of arcane knowledge, all cut out of coloured paper, housed old Miss Pyefinch, the postmistress, who read fortunes for a shilling, with an express service for juveniles at sixpence. Other ladies stood at small tables, inviting speculation as to the number of beans in a bottle, or the precise weight (in his clothes as he stood, and including the grey bowler) of no less a person than Owain Allington Esquire himself.

'Jolly good idea, eh?' There was unenvious admiration in Wilfred Osborne's voice as he commented on this last invitation. 'Go down very well. They'll weigh him, you know, right at the end, when the prizes and so forth are being announced. And he'll make quite a thing of it. No condescension, a friendly air, dignity nicely maintained all the same – and at the announcement they'll all clap and he'll take off that hat to them. Then he'll have a word with one old woman, and a word with another old woman, and walk back to the house and disappear. And there it's understood that the quality join him for a glass of sherry. We'll have to go, I'm afraid.' Osborne paused. 'It does recall old times to me, I'm bound to say.'

Appleby had listened to this little speech with interest. It seemed to have been spoken in perfect charity. But had it been sharpened – surely a little beyond Osborne's common command of language – by something deep down in the man?

'Oh, look!' Judith said. 'They're going to have the opening. I'm so glad we're in time for it.'

'It's old Bertha Killcanon. She was younger than my mother, but a great friend of hers.' Osborne was silent for a moment. 'Take careful note, Judith. It will probably be your turn next year.'

'Judith's already a connoisseur,' Appleby said. 'That's why we had to be early. She collects these occasions. I suppose it's in the interest of a little book. A monograph which will come out at the same time as the one she says I'm going to write on bee-keeping. *One Hundred and One Ways to Open Charity Bazaars.*'

Lady Killcanon had advanced with Owain Allington to a small platform. The Reverend Adrian Scrape ('MA Oxon.' Appleby had remarked on the church notice-board) walked a pace behind, rather as if about to provide the consolations of religion to some illustrious victim of the scaffold. Lady Killcanon smiled graciously to right and left, and one almost expected her to make, with her gloved right hand, the little seesaw motion which used to be as much as royalty judged dignified in the way of a wave. But Lady Killcanon, of course, did not do this, since she perfectly knew her place. It was the place of a very grand Edwardian lady, who had written speeches for her papa the Foreign Secretary to deliver in the House of Lords, and who had no intention of merely stumbling through a few artless words now. Lady Killcanon, who was dressed with exaggerated old lady's femininity in a multiplicity of filmy and fluttering garments, raised a bony face to the heavens and in a strong masculine voice entered upon an anatomy of the current political situation. Allington stood on one side of her, looking thoughtful and instructed. Mr Scrape stood on the other, clearly aware of himself as smiling fixedly. Actually, Mr Scrape was boiling with impatience, since there was already seething in him that master-passion which he had to repress (because of his cloth) during three hundred and sixty-four days of the year. Below, the commonality stood properly attentive and silent – except that on their outskirts, two or three infants-in-arms, as yet unacquainted with the ordinances of English society, kept up an unseasonable wailing. Only William Goodcoal, who cherished the insane dream of piping radio and television through all the hundred and twelve principal apartments of Killcanon Court, kept shouting 'Hear! hear!' very loudly, in the secure conviction that this would recommend him to the favourable notice of the speaker.

'And finally' – Lady Killcanon said after some fifteen minutes – 'let me remind you (and I know that it need be no more than that) of the words which my late father – '

'Hear! Hear!' This time, William Goodcoal flourished a small Union Jack, hastily snatched from the grasp of his son and heir.

' – of the words which my late father uttered in the Upper Chamber upon the occasion of the Third Imperial Conference in London – which took place, as we all know, from the 15th of April to the 14th of May, 1907 – '

'Hear! Hear! Hurrar for her Ladyship!'

' "*Let nation speak peace unto nation*" – these were my father's magnificent words – "*and let a despicable administration resign forthwith*".' Lady Killcanon paused impressively. 'Ladies and gentlemen, I have great pleasure in declaring your beautiful new hall open.'

There was a moment's bewildered silence. Among those present, the more impressionable even raised their eyes and looked about them, as if expecting that at this august personage's summons, as at the decree of Kubla Khan, some stately pleasure-dome should at once create itself in air. Mr Goodcoal, however, saved the situation.

'Hurrar for her Ladyship!' shouted Mr Goodcoal. 'Hip, hip, hurrar for Lady Killcanon, God bless her!'

Adequate cheering ensued. Little Alice Mellors (the keeper's daughter), a born exhibitionist who had been straining at the leash for some time, marched perkily forward and presented Lady Killcanon with a bouquet. Owain Allington proposed a vote of thanks. Mr Scrape seconded it with becoming brevity. The fête had begun.

6

The dog Rasselas, Appleby noticed, was bearing a dignified part in the proceedings. He had accompanied the personages of principal consideration to their platform. Now, with a money-box strapped to his back, he was moving purposively among the company at large. Rasselas was an almost depressingly well-trained dog, and his technique in the cause of charitable endeavour was simple and effective. He simply came to a halt dead in front of you. If you took evasive action, he made a little detour of his own and then planted himself firmly in your path once more. Determined that there should be no mistake about buying himself off, Appleby produced a florin, held it firmly before the creature's nose, and then dropped it as noisily as possible into the box. Rasselas gave him a polite nod and walked away. And he showed no further interest in Appleby during the remainder of the afternoon.

Judith had been detected by Lady Killcanon, and constrained to form part of her *entourage* as she made her ritual round of the several stalls. Although Lady Killcanon appeared now to be under the impression that she had just successfully launched a liner ('And God bless all who sail in her,' she had said suddenly to the astonished Mrs Pecover the cow-man's wife), she preserved a marked acuity as a purchaser – holding up jars of jam firmly to the light, and further bewildering Mrs Pecover by referring to her gingerbread as parliament-cake and questioning her closely about the ingredients. Appleby felt it justifiable to slip away from this progress. Judith would no doubt buy more than enough of this and that to uphold the reputation of Long Dream.

As he made a general survey of the scene, he found it hard not to feel something slightly uncanny in its complete transformation from the night before. All that was left of the whole elaborate lay-out of the *son et lumière* was, so to speak, a shadowy presence constituted by various trodden or discoloured areas of the turf. And now, rapidly obliterating even that, was this harmless jamboree. Would its paraphernalia, in turn, be cleared away as expeditiously? The marquee and some of the tents would presumably stand until the following morning. What if there was a dead body in one of them by then?

This bizarre speculation brought Appleby to a halt. It is not thus that the imaginations of retired policemen are accustomed to start into activity. There must really be something sinister in the atmosphere of Allington to put such an idea into his head. And yet, quite clearly, there was nothing of the kind. Over there was Owain Allington, a modest country squire going to some trouble to keep up a traditional relationship with his simpler neighbours and their kind. Even his grey bowler fitting in quite well – particularly with Lady Killcanon, whose papa had probably worn one on informal occasions. And a little farther away was the former squire, Wilfred Osborne, perfectly easy in not the easiest of situations. Osborne was, of course, all right with the gentry; whether or not he still owned a park and a manor and hunters and a trout-stream was nothing to them, and if he was sociably disposed he certainly needn't go without a single invitation he had formerly received. But with the village people and the small tenants it was rather different; no doubt they preserved the sterling virtues of the folk, but it was equally certain that they experienced honest satisfaction at the spectacle of a former oppressor fallen into near-indigence. Not that Osborne had really been an oppressor; quite obviously, there was nothing of the sort in his nature. Still, he had owned the broad estates and the hall; and he was a fair target for mild malice in consequence. But then Osborne knew this perfectly well, as any countryman must do. He would also be aware – even if not in a consciously formulated way – that it was only one component in an attitude as complex as anything centuries-old must be. He was having a very good time now, talking to all and sundry. No, it was improbable that in that direction there lay anything sinister at all.

What was troubling Appleby – it suddenly came to him quite clearly – was the man who had died. And it wasn't just the fact of the man's death, or even the macabre unaccountability of its circumstances. It was rather the manner in which it seemed to have been swept rapidly into oblivion. Where was the man's body now? Presumably in some county mortuary, awaiting or undergoing post-mortem. Just where had he died? Appleby found he couldn't even exactly place the position of that unlikely glass box. And who was he? Appleby experienced an unaccountable impatience to find out about this. Allington would have the answer; he must have been kept informed – even on this busy day he must have been kept informed – of any facts that had come to light. Appleby looked round for the grey bowler, and found himself confronting a green trilby instead. It was on the head of Colonel Pride – Tommy Pride, according to Osborne – the Chief Constable.

Appleby recalled with dismay having committed himself to the statement that he didn't care for Pride. He wasn't in the habit of saying that sort of thing – and why should he say it about this particular chap? Pride was a quiet man, military-looking but not obtrusively so, with a close-cropped moustache and close-cropped, carefully brushed hair. This last fact was apparent because Pride had now taken off his hat to Appleby – a gesture intended to acknowledge, perhaps in a slightly chilly way, the fact that Appleby had held a job more exalted than, if not exactly comparable with, his own. Appleby, of course, took off his hat in turn. He wanted to say, with reference to the rustic populace surrounding them, 'And a pretty pair of Charlies we must look.' He was inhibited partly by suspecting that Pride might find this a mysterious remark, and partly because he had just noticed that his own hat was a green trilby too. Moreover

Pride's tweeds were very like his own tweeds, and Pride's stature was precisely his. If, after the ceremonial weighing of Owain Allington Esquire, he and Pride were to mount the scale in turn, it was unlikely that there would turn out to be a couple of pounds between them.

Colonel Pride looked distrustfully at Sir John Appleby, and Sir John Appleby looked distrustfully at Colonel Pride. It was possible that to each the same thought had come in the same moment. But it probably came to Appleby in rather more picturesque form. If he and Pride, he was thinking, were to hunch themselves down on each side of a fireplace, the effect would be very much that of those twinned china dogs still frequently to be found guarding the hearths of the good poor. More learnedly put, here was his *Doppelgänger.* No wonder he didn't care for Tommy Pride.

'Afternoon, Appleby,' Colonel Pride said.

'How are you, Pride?' Appleby said. 'Very pleasant show.'

'Very pleasant. Nice afternoon for it.'

There was a moment's silence.

'Good turn out,' Appleby said. 'People from all over the place.'

'Car park full.' Colonel Pride paused, as if about to move on. Instead, he made quite a long speech. 'They go through the house – the people who have come some way in cars. Half-a-crown. The locals don't, of course. They've satisfied their curiosity long ago. A great bore, having people trailing through your rooms, I'd think. Decent of Allington. No call to. Simply for charity, and so forth. Nothing to do with income tax. Treats my people very well, too, I gather. I send in a couple of men, you know, to help keep an eye on the spoons and forks. Always have to have a dinner-table elaborately laid – have you noticed? – when you open up your place like that. And I advised him against hiring private-eye fellows. Heard some very bad things about them. Planting the appearance of pilfering on perfectly innocent half-crowners, you know, just to gain a bonus. We don't want any of those city rackets down here.'

'Extremely wise of you, if I may say so.' Appleby fancied he was conscious of people glancing curiously at Pride and himself. Perhaps they were making jokes about Tweedledum and Tweedledee. He himself must be careful to see that these two didn't have a battle. He was determined to get some information out of Pride, all the same. And presumably Pride *had* information. Chief Constables are not invariably well clued up on the passing scene within their jurisdiction. But Pride couldn't have failed to acquaint himself with what had happened on the previous night at Allington Park. He must know about Appleby's own odd implication in it. Indeed, it would scarcely be possible for him not to refer to it. So Appleby refrained from prompting. And, sure enough, Pride came to the point.

'That business here last night,' he said. 'Poor show. Awkward thing. Sorry you tumbled into it. Odd, in a way, that it should have been you. Coals to Newcastle, I mean.' Pride paused for a moment, as if rather dimly trying to verify the appositeness of this figure of speech. 'Lucky for Allington, though. To have had your support, that is.'

'I left as soon as your people arrived and I'd told them anything I could. Naturally, the inquiry wasn't far advanced at that point. The chap hadn't been identified. Allington felt he'd never set eyes on him.'

'Identified? Ah, yes – important that. Investigation going on, of course.'

'Of course.'

It was an impasse, since Pride now seemed to feel that he had said what was necessary. Appleby was constrained to risk at least a sighting shot.

'The *son et lumière* people have got their junk away pretty smartly,' he said.

'Needed it elsewhere, no doubt.'

'That may be it – and Allington was anxious it should go. Before the affair this afternoon, that is. I see they've even taken the control-room, or whatever they call it. The place in which we found the body.'

'We haven't got a murder on our hands, you know.' Pride had stiffened. 'Would you expect me to object?'

'To the removal?' For a second Appleby hesitated, considering the precise form of words Pride had just used. It seemed illuminating – and Appleby decided to take a risk. 'Yes,' he said. 'I would. But you didn't have a chance.'

'Unless I have occasion to hold an inquiry and deliver a reprimand, I take full responsibility for any decision arrived at by one of my officers.'

'Yes, of course. And this particular decision *was* taken by one of your – '

'Really, I don't think that the affairs of the County Constabulary are any concern – ' Rather surprisingly, Pride checked himself. 'Sorry,' he said. 'Relation of confidence should subsist between us, I hope you feel. And, of course, you're quite right.'

'Allington must have been rather urgent about it, I imagine. And one of your subordinates would be a good deal more impressed by a local magnate than you or I should be. It wasn't unnatural either, that Allington should want the thing out of the way before this show.'

'No.' Pride appeared not altogether happy with this conclusion on the matter. 'Don't think I'm not concerned about it, Appleby. Mind you, my people worked on it intensively from an early hour this morning. They excluded foul play. If there were any suspicion of *that*, of course, we'd be judged to have fallen down on the job. In letting the damned thing be taken away, that is.'

'I take it the dead man has *not* been identified so far?'

'Not when I was last in touch with anyone. It rather tells against his being a local, don't you think? And one's pretty sure what happened. Not quite a tramp – they say he didn't look quite like a tramp – but a fellow drifting across country for one reason or another. Been walking all day – '

'His shoes didn't suggest that to me.'

'His shoes?' Colonel Pride was disconcerted; it was as if he had forgotten Appleby's eye-witness status. 'Well, it's not essential to the argument. He was benighted, and that scared him. Suggests a townee, wouldn't you say? It's remarkable how reluctant fellows of that sort are to spend even a summer night under the stars. So he climbed up into this affair as the only available shelter, fell asleep on the floor, rolled over and dislodged something, and this live cable got him. Trouble brewing for somebody in the *son et lumière* business, I suspect. But nothing beyond that. The coroner will sit on the poor chap, and that will be the end of it.'

'You're very probably right.' Appleby judged it was time to be soothing. 'The only thing I'm not confident about is his not being a local man. The time has been rather short to be sure of that. When a question of this sort turns up in any district, whether urban or rural, it's astonishing how many respectable male characters turn out to be away from home and unaccounted for.'

'Perfectly true.'

'Of course, when the news of an unidentified dead body gets around, people become scared, and turn up with admissions about missing relatives. Until that happens, they keep dark about a husband or son having a night or two out. And the news of this affair must just be beginning to get around the district now.'

'That's certainly so.' Colonel Pride was perturbed. 'And it's hard to see why a man should climb into that damned thing if he had a perfectly respectable roof of his own near by.'

'I quite agree, Pride. I've thought about it a little – you must forgive me if I do that – and only one possible explanation has come to me so far.' Appleby was glancing here and there in the crowd. 'Do you happen to know a citizen called William Goodcoal?'

'Never heard of him. Sounds like a fellow in a book.'

'You've heard *from* him. He was the man who did all that enthusiastic bellowing while the old lady was making her speech. Bellowing is rather his line. He has a machine over in that van which will bellow as loud as you please. I'm going over to have a word with him now.'

7

Lady Killcanon having departed with her bouquet and her frugal and judicious purchases in an ancient Rolls-Royce, Owain Allington felt it proper to give a little undivided attention to the woman of next consequence now left on the scene.

'Don't you think we might take a turn down the terrace, Lady Appleby, and return refreshed to the fracas? We've done not too badly, I'd say, on the first round.'

Judith accepted the invitation; she wasn't averse to bettering her acquaintance with Allington, whom she hadn't very frequently met. His mere manner interested her, for one thing. She told herself that he always exhibited a shade more confidence than there was any call for. It couldn't basically be the product of social uncertainty, although she had once or twice previously heard him talk in a way that almost deliberately suggested something like that. It was much more likely to reflect a sense that he had made a bad guess about himself when he dropped a distinguished scientific career for his present way of life.

She had known similar things happen before. Or at least she could recall one or two cases of men making their way in exacting and absorbing professions – as lawyers, surgeons, scholars – who had unexpectedly 'come into property', as the phrase was, and thrown up their jobs in consequence. It hadn't, in her experience, worked well, since an able man, after all, can't delude himself that there is any hard challenge in pottering around an estate. Even so, there had been an element of piety in these cases. An elder brother had died, or something of that sort, and what must be thought of as some peculiarly English *mystique* had come into play. In Allington's case the *mystique* had been the odd one of a quite distant family history. Somehow or other he had made rather a lot of money rather quickly, and he had sunk it in this business of becoming, so to speak, an Allington again. Imaginatively, there was no doubt something attractive about it. He must be an unstable creature, all the same.

'Has all this been a success?' Judith asked. 'Do you like it?'

'Life here?' If Allington was a little startled by this directness of address, he was too intelligent to pretend to be at a loss. 'I don't think I know yet. They say, of course, that as a physicist I was feeling the twitch of my tether, and that I took the chance of a break when it came. It's a reasonable conjecture. I was rather good. There's no denying I was rather good. But, as you know, it's young men who make the running in my sort of thing. Even more than with the poets, and characters of that sort. Year by year, the neurones inside one's skull become less numerous. And what is affected, oddly enough, appears to be the mind's more intuitive operations. And physics and maths are damnably intuitive – beyond a modest bread-and-butter level, that is. When that fails, we have to be turfed out into being heads of this and that – like those wise and worried old father-figures, sitting behind desks and directing unfathomable researches by vast teams of young eggheads, that you get in television drama.'

'I see.' Judith had a fleeting impression that she had been listening to a set piece; that it wasn't only once or twice before that Allington had gone into this explanatory routine. 'But you still do some scientific work?'

'I must confess that I conduct a little experiment from time to time.' Allington paused for a moment. 'By the way, I was so sorry to run your husband into the business of that unfortunate discovery last night.'

'I hardly think it worried him, such affairs, after all, used to be very much in his day's work.'

'But I'm afraid I gave him a dull evening as well. I'd rather expected my nephew Martin to turn up after dinner. But he didn't. Indeed, he hasn't turned up yet, although other members of my family have. Three nieces *plus* two husbands – as I think I told Sir John. And several of their children, as well. I very much hope you will meet them.'

Judith offered a civil reply, although she wasn't very sure that she really wanted to embrace the acquaintance of shoals of further Allingtons. Her host had now conducted her round a corner of the terrace, and they were passing a light barrier to which had been affixed a notice saying PRIVATE. Allington regarded this dubiously.

'I wonder whether that looks a bit unfriendly?' he said. 'After all, all these good people are my guests for the afternoon, more or less. But tiresome things can happen, if they roam all over the place. Things vanish from the greenhouses, and the gardeners are upset.'

Judith again produced an appropriate murmur. Allington, she felt, rather abounded in nice feelings. But now she noticed that his attention had strayed for a moment, and that he appeared to be listening to the miscellaneous hubbub from the other side of the house. William Goodcoal's canned music was its chief component. But the assembled children were also yelling fairly pertinaciously, and for a moment there had been the sound of a motor engine. It was this that Allington proved to have been held by.

'I thought it might be Martin's car,' he said. 'He'd ignore the car park, of course, and drive straight up to the house. But it isn't. I'd know the sound of Martin's damned car anywhere.'

'Why is it damned?' Judith had detected the inflection of something almost grim in Allington's voice. 'Is it abominably noisy?'

'It's abominably powerful. And Martin drives it far too fast. He treats a common English high road as if it were the *Autostrada del Sole.*'

'It's against the law to do quite that sort of speeding now.'

'Quite so. Plenty of people do it, of course.' Allington hesitated. 'If the boy got himself disqualified, and was off the road for a time, I'd be easier in my mind.'

'Is Martin just a boy?'

'Well, no. In fact, rather far from it. But I think of him that way. As I was telling your husband, Martin will inherit Allington one day. Good for him, I hope – a settled country life.'

'I see.' What, in fact, Judith thought she saw was an answer to her own earlier speculation. Allington was devoted to his nephew. So much so, that he was mounting this whole country-gentleman business in his interest. Martin Allington had to be rescued from something – and presumably from something even more hazardous than driving a powerful car much too fast. And the rescue was to be effected by handing him Allington Park and its attendant position of consideration in this eminently respectable county. It was a plan almost certainly belonging to that class of fond plans which come to nothing. For the first time, Judith felt an impulse of sympathy towards this slightly factitious squire before whose mansion she was perambulating. 'It's a wonderful thing to have to offer anybody,' she said.

'I think he'll do very well.' Allington, who had spoken almost gruffly, hesitated again. 'He hits the bottle,' he said suddenly.

For a moment, Judith's feeling of sympathy wavered. She didn't know Owain Allington at all well, and this sudden confidence was rather forcing the pace. Moreover, it hadn't been of an order to which there is any easy reply. Judith chose a somewhat modish one.

'Better that than drugs, I suppose,' she said.

'That depends on the drug.' The grim note in Allington's voice was now indubitable. 'Hard drinking isn't too bad in itself. But ahead of it lies alcoholism – an addiction one doesn't care to think about.' He glanced at Judith, and seemed to realize that he had plunged rather oddly into this family matter. 'Your husband and I happened just to touch on this last night,' he said. 'It turned out he had met Martin – I didn't gather just how – and seemed to know about this liability of his. At least, that's the impression I got. And I imagined he might have mentioned it to you. Otherwise I wouldn't have started in on such a boring matter. First a corpse in the gazebo, and then a skeleton in the cupboard. I'm really not serving the Applebys at all well.' Allington came to a halt. 'The castle looks rather impressive from here, don't you think?'

Judith agreed about the impressiveness of the castle. It had been quite time that her host changed the subject. Not – she told herself honestly – that she hadn't asked for what she'd got. For wasn't she much given to vulgar curiosity? Wasn't it the motive, for instance, of her wanting John to worry out the not terribly interesting mystery of last night's dead man? But now she thought of an innocuous topic which ought to last Allington and herself until they returned to the scene of the fête.

'Wilfred Osborne came to lunch,' she said, 'before we drove him over here. We talked about the story of the Allington treasure – because of its having been mentioned, you know, in your *son et lumière*. I think I have a theory about it.'

'A theory about it!' Allington was quite startled. 'I've heard plenty of theories from time to time. But I'm sure, Lady Appleby, that yours will be a particularly interesting one.'

'I think it was dug up by Humphrey Repton when he was improving the place. He improved himself on the side.'

'There! I told you so!' Allington was a little more than adequately delighted. 'And nobody has thought of it before. Repton's people must have dug up acres and acres of the park – creating a new rise here and a new vale there, grove to nod to grove, and all the perspectives and side-screens and distances as they should be. Look at all that tolerably mature timber. There's hardly a tree that doesn't stand where it does because Humphrey Repton pointed a directing finger at the spot. Clearly he found the treasure, slipped it into his waistcoat-pocket, and made off with it. How cross the first Mr Osborne of Allington would have been if he'd known.'

'Would it have been legally his, if Mr Repton hadn't got away with it?'

'I've no idea.' Allington laughed easily. 'And I've no idea what the position would be if the unlikely stuff were found today. What they call treasure-trove, I suppose. Morally, it ought to belong to the Queen.' They were now retracing their steps along the terrace. 'Or perhaps to some Stuart pretender. Is there one still? How ignorant one is!'

'I wonder why it's believed to be in the park?' Judith was determined to make the subject last out until they had rejoined the crowd. 'The castle, surely, was being closely invested by the parliamentary army. If something had to be buried, wouldn't it have to be within the walls of the castle itself?'

'Probably too risky. If it was known to exist, the Roundheads would have ransacked the place before setting fire to it. You'd decide it was more hopeful to creep through their lines in the night, and bury it where they'd never think.'

'Or get it right away by wagon or on horseback?'

'I don't like that idea at all. It spoils the fun.'

'Very well. They simply dropped it in the lake. Much quicker and quieter than digging a great hole and then obliterating all traces of it in the dark. And the stuff would be gold and silver. It wouldn't come to any harm.'

'There wasn't much of a lake then.' Allington was suddenly quite serious. 'But I suppose there was quite enough for the purpose. The stuff would be in a chest or something, one imagines, and that would be deep in mud now, and probably rotted away. But the metal – gold and silver, as you say – would simply – ' He broke off. 'Lady Appleby, what kids we are!'

'Yes, indeed. But I'll feel more grown-up when I've paid my half-crown and had some tea.'

'Don't soak yourself in it,' Allington said. 'There's prescriptively a glass of sherry afterwards in the drawing-room. But I shouldn't be positively astounded if it turned out to be a reasonable sort of champagne.'

'That sounds wonderful.' In fact, Judith thought it didn't. A glass of champagne – not a particularly momentous object – best appears unheralded. 'But oughtn't you to keep it for the grand celebration?' she asked.

'But so I am. We celebrate the departure of all those worthy people, and the return of a year's peace to Allington.'

'I wasn't thinking of that. I was thinking of the moment when you draw up all that lost wealth from the lake.'

'Ah, yes – that will be a moment, certainly.' Suddenly Owain Allington quickened his pace. 'We mustn't be too late for old Mrs Junkin's meringues,' he said. 'Although I shouldn't be surprised if she's kept one or two back for myself and partner.'

'I shouldn't be surprised, either,' Judith said.

8

Appleby had bought a television set from William Goodcoal, and the proprietor of the Public Address System consequently received him with considerable respect – even going so far as to facilitate conversation by turning down the volume of the musical entertainment being discoursed from his van. Appleby was not in the same class as Lady Killcanon, and Mr Goodcoal would have been surprised to hear himself leading a cheer for him. But the gentleman at Long Dream paid his bills (which was more than the previous occupants, relations of the gentleman's wife, had been able to do) and had a handle to his name: a combination of circumstances which Mr Goodcoal, a right-thinking man, accounted at its proper worth. Moreover it was agreeable in Sir John Appleby to come over and have a chat with him. Mr Goodcoal was glad to observe that Mrs Goodcoal (who had been a little put out as a consequence of being asked to wash tea-cups rather than hand them round) was so located as to have this distinguishing circumstance within her view.

'A skilled job you have here, Mr Goodcoal,' Appleby said, after having exchanged salutations. 'A good many things to think of at once. I'm surprised you haven't had to bring along one or two of your assistants. But no doubt you have plenty for them all to do.' William Goodcoal, he hoped, was properly gratified by this unblushing conjuring up of a mythical corps of subordinates.

'Well, sir, I won't say the order books are not pretty full. And as for working single-handed – well, it's the expertise that counts. That and the up-to-date character of the equipment, sir. Goodcoal Enterprises insist on having nothing but the best and latest thing. As far as this part of the country goes, I think I may say we are very competitive, Sir John – very competitive, indeed. And the same is true of our associated companies.' Mr Goodcoal paused in order to make a hasty grab at one of the dials in front of him. A rather unpleasant wailing sound (as of a woman in trouble over a demon lover) had suddenly begun to issue from the antique loud-speakers above his head.

'A very good tone, you have there,' Appleby said. 'A nice quality of sound. An excellent *timbre*. I've been hearing some criticism, in that field, of this big affair Mr Allington has had here during the last few weeks. Very coarse reproduction at times, it seems. The wiring all wrong. Synchronization defective. Fluctuating volume. Oscillation. Interference. Poor show.'

'They've no conscience, them big London firms.' Mr Goodcoal had given a snort of gratified contempt. 'And no personal supervision. Now, sir, with Goodcoal Enterprises all installations are under the direct superintendence of the proprietor.'

'I'm sure they are.'

'Or the Managing Director, Sir John.' If not very logically, William Goodcoal's imagination was taking wing. 'Or of the Chairman of the Board… Drat that thing!' The machine in front of Mr Goodcoal had begun to emit loops and coils of magnetic tape in a displeasing fashion, and as a consequence something like an air-raid warning was sounding over the alarmed heads of the mild revellers in Allington Park. 'Interval,' William Goodcoal said resourcefully, and flicked a switch. An obedient silence fell.

'I suppose, Mr Goodcoal, that you have a great many young lads eager to come into your business?' Appleby spoke diffidently; he might have had several junior Applebys at Dream for whose apprenticeship to an honest trade he was beginning anxiously to cast around.

'Queues of them, Sir John. I can absolutely take my pick among the school leavers.' Mr Goodcoal's imagination again soared. 'All the most brilliant minds, sir, in Linger Secondary Modern. And I have the ear of the headmaster, Sir John. He knows where there is a future for his lads. Take it from me.'

'I'm delighted to hear you say so.' Appleby was in fact a little tired of taking it. 'Boys can get quite mad about everything electrical. But what about rather older men, Mr Goodcoal? Are there any real enthusiasts in Linger, or round about?'

This was a topic upon which Mr Goodcoal proved to have much to say. Mr Goodcoal acted in an advisory capacity to numerous amateurs (some of them deep scholars, with letters after their names) as far afield as Snarl and even King's Yatter. Others, of more humble station, were glad of corporate instruction once a week under the auspices of the local education authority. It was interesting work, responsible work. Lady Killcanon herself had spoken to him about it on the occasion when she did him the honour of calling him out to her car to fit a new battery in her electric torch (previously supplied by Goodcoal Enterprises Limited).

'Are any of them eccentrics?' Appleby asked.

'None has ever mentioned it to me,' Mr Goodcoal produced this reply after considerable thought. 'Church, mostly, Sir John. My own connexion is largely Church. But, of course, there are Methodists and Baptists too.'

'I see.' Appleby betrayed no discomposure before this. When he next spoke, it was with the air of starting quite a different branch of the subject for discussion. 'I suppose, Mr Goodcoal, there must be some without the intellectual equipment to tackle a difficult science like yours? Who get out of their depth, I mean.'

'There do be that, sir.' When aiming at *gravitas*, Mr Goodcoal's idiom tended to turn rural. 'And a tragedy it be to be observing of. That natural, now.'

'A natural?' Forty years of this sort of thing had taught Appleby's scalp to tingle at the right moment. It tingled now. 'Which would that be? Young Pescod? Or Mrs Pumphry's boy? Or Billy Bubwith who's always idling about the green at Drool?'

'None of these, sir. None of these. Knockdown, Sir John.'

'Knockdown?' For a moment Appleby failed to acknowledge in this vocable a feasible surname even of the most rustic sort. 'Somebody *called* Knockdown?'

'Leofranc Knockdown, sir.'

'Dear me! I haven't heard of him.' It seemed to Appleby that anyone so circumstanced in infancy as to emerge from it thus denominated could scarcely hope to have full possession of his faculties. 'And he's a natural?'

'Simple, Sir John – simple, without a doubt. What the powers and wonders of electricity mean to Knockdown is no more, you might say, than sparks and flashes. He'll do himself a mischief one day, mark my words.'

'Is he in his mid-twenties, and with ginger hair?'

'Ah, you've seen him around.'

'Does he live with his family? Is he capable of looking after himself?'

'He lodges with a couple of the name of Clamtree, just outside Linger on the Potton road. There's somebody pays something, if you ask me.' Mr Goodcoal had lowered his voice to the pitch in which it is appropriate to speak of improper matters. 'A bastard, sir, I'd say.'

'Would these Clamtrees miss him quickly?'

'I'd reckon not.' Mr Goodcoal, although his mind seemed marked by no great rapidity of movement, was beginning to look surprised. 'Knockdown gets a bit of work here and a bit of work there, you see, and there will be times when he thinks a barn a good enough place to sleep in. And they do say his trouble waxes and wanes with the moon.'

'Rather a lonely fellow, and with this obsession with electricity?'

'Just that. Neither father, mother or brother that any ever heard of.'

'Perhaps that's just as well, Mr Goodcoal. Because I'm afraid poor Leofranc Knockdown is dead.'

'I suppose we can pack up now?' Appleby asked hopefully. It was half-an-hour later, and he had succeeded in finding his wife.

'Good gracious, no!' Judith gave every appearance of registering shock. 'It wouldn't do at all.'

'That old woman went away.'

'That's quite different. People who declare fêtes and sales and bazaars open always clear out early. It's part of the ritual.'

'Bother the ritual. I've discharged my mission.'

'What do you mean – your mission?'

'You know perfectly well what I mean. You dragged me over here to poke officiously into the great gazebo mystery. Well, I've poked – and naturally it's a mystery no longer. I've just got to find your friend Tommy Pride' – Appleby said this with considerable satisfaction – 'in order to offer him a helpful word, and after that we can find Wilfred Osborne and clear out.'

'John – you mean you know who the dead man was, and how he came to be killed?'

'Yes, of course. He was the only thing he *could* be – as I saw clearly enough. A poor fellow who was mad about every sort of electrical gadgetry, but in a dim-witted – actually a mentally subnormal – way. He climbed into the wretched affair to glut himself with gaping, actually got to crawling around, and was unlucky enough to be killed instantaneously on the high-voltage part of the affair. He has no near relations, I'm glad to say.'

'I thought it must be something like that.'

'You did nothing of the kind. Or at least you didn't *say* you did.' Appleby was looking at his wife balefully. 'In fact, you as good as announced that this fellow Allington had contrived some fiendish sort of murder.'

'That was only a hypothesis.' Judith appeared to feel that this dismissed the matter. 'But, talking of Mr Allington, he's had old Mrs Junkin keep you a meringue.'

'I haven't the slightest yearning for one of old Mrs Junkin's meringues.'

'Perhaps that's just as well.' Judith was glancing over her shoulder. 'There's a long queue now, and you couldn't very well jump it. Mr Scrape's first session must be over. Yes, they're still coming out of the marquee. But there will be more Bingo in half-an-hour. That's when we'll go.'

'Bingo! Do you mean to say that the Reverend Mr Scrape's gambling hell is nothing but a Bingo palace?'

'Of course. But he's said to be fearfully good at it, and quite to live for it from year to year. For one thing, it's the only occasion on which he sees crowded rows of his parishioners in front of him. And there's a strong ritual element in it, after all. You'll see when we go. We'll take Wilfred too.'

'Judith, I will *not* sit under this dissolute priest for the purpose – '

'Do be quiet, John. Here is Mr Scrape coming to talk to us.'

Mr Scrape advanced upon the Applebys, cordially smiling and energetically mopping his brow. He was a cleric of the stringy sort, such as one scarcely expects to drip at every pore. But it was this that he seemed to be doing. It would be very hot inside the marquee, and the deep Anglican calm which must characterize his common sacerdotal occasions was probably a poor preparation for the altogether more exigent patter required of him upon this red-letter day of his year. Now that he had emerged into the open air, Mr Scrape gave no hint of anything manic in his personality. His manner was bland. And he addressed Appleby, to whom he had already been introduced, in so soothing a fashion that Appleby almost taxed himself with evincing some unmotivated nervous agitation.

'My dear Sir John, I quite failed to say how kindly I take your supporting our small annual occasion. Lady Appleby, I hope you are not too fatigued, and that you have not overburdened yourself with our good friends' jellies and jams. My own little contribution is now half-made, but presently I must return to the marquee for one further session. A beautiful afternoon, but almost oppressively warm. Might we take a stroll, perhaps, by the side of the lake – and towards the castle? Mr Allington very kindly allows the older village boys to swim there, and I think it may be wise just to survey the scene. One does not want Mr Allington's hospitality abused by anything rowdy. Innocent skylarking is in order, of course. They may not, by the way, all have bathing-slips, Lady Appleby.'

'I don't think I'll feel myself disturbed.'

'Quite so, quite so. How fortunate we are that there is so little unwholesome prudery nowadays! And the human body is a temple, after all. Lady Appleby, pray remark the step.'

Judith remarked the step. It seemed cooler by the lake, and a little breeze appeared to be moving with the slow current from its farther end. There were one or two small groups of people among the castle ruins; no doubt they were recuperating from the excitement of the fête. From somewhere ahead came sounds of shouting and splashing, and behind them they could still hear the unwearying efforts of Mr Goodcoal's Public Address System.

'How good it is of Mr Allington to let us intrude upon his privacy in this way!' Mr Scrape said. He seemed given to pious ejaculation of this sort. 'A man with a high sense of public duty, and always willing to give time and thought to his neighbours. It is a sign of true greatness, surely, when one of strong intellectual endowment has a care for trivial and humble things.' Mr Scrape paused to assist Judith courteously over a low stile. 'And so delightful a family! For nephews and nieces may be held to constitute a family, I think, when they are so closely attached to an uncle as in this instance. Sir John, pray avoid the cow-pat.'

Appleby avoided the cow-pat. He hoped that Judith's sense of the ridiculous was not going to prompt her to some unsuitable response to the small-talk of this terrible clerical toady. For that seemed to be what the Reverend Mr Scrape was. Indeed, it was almost possible to say that it was what Mr Scrape gave himself out to be. Appleby found himself wondering fleetingly whether there might not be something rather deep about the Vicar of Allington. But however that might be, Judith was fortunately behaving herself.

'I've heard of Martin Allington,' she said. 'But it seems he hasn't come.'

'Mr Martin Allington is expected hourly.' Mr Scrape gave a great effect of weight to this announcement. 'Hourly,' he repeated. 'And I greatly hope it may be before our small festivities close. It is well known that he is to be Mr Allington's heir. And this renders him doubly welcome among us.'

'But some other relations have arrived? John and I haven't met them yet.'

'You will.' Mr Scrape produced this with confidence and quiet fervour, rather as if he were offering ghostly assurance to a dying parishioner. 'Miss Hope Allington, and also the Lethbridges and the Barfords with their delightful children, are already here. They are mingling with us in their customary unassuming way. And, as you know, Mr Allington invites us to meet his household over a glass of wine when all these good people have gone away. Not that one must think of hastening their departure. Only I shall be glad, I own, when there is an end to the musical entertainment provided by the worthy Goodcoal. You know Goodcoal, Sir John?'

'Yes, I've been talking to him.' A thought struck Appleby. 'By the way, Mr Scrape, I don't know how the bounds of your parish run. But would a man with the odd name of Leofranc Knockdown, living somewhere on the Potton side of Linger, be one of your flock?'

'Ah, no. That is in a neighbouring parish. Potton-cum-Outreach. Nevertheless, I know the man. A simple fellow – scarcely with all his wits, indeed. But willing and reliable, entirely reliable. He has trimmed my hedges before now.'

'I am sorry to say it was he who was found dead here last night.'

'God rest his soul. I have, of course, heard about an accident. I believe it was yourself, Sir John, and Mr Allington – ?'

'Yes, it was.'

'Sad, very sad. And a great shock for Mr Allington.'

'Not more than for my husband,' Judith said. 'Mr Allington didn't know this dead man from Adam.'

'Ah, I see.' Mr Scrape had come to a sudden halt. The bathers were now visible, and he might have been assuring himself that no impropriety of demeanour or posture was to be obtruded by them on Lady Appleby's refined regard. 'I don't know whether the unfortunate event has yet been made generally known. Will it be necessary, Sir John, to hold an inquest over the poor fellow?'

'Most certainly it will.'

'And there will be what is called an open verdict?'

'I hardly suppose so.' Appleby was surprised. 'Death by misadventure will be the obvious conclusion.'

'But surely it was very strange that this poor man – '

'Not when one knows about certain of his interests. Perfectly innocent interests, I may say.' Appleby spoke a shade impatiently. He felt that he had had enough of the Knockdown affair. 'A very nice bathing-place, I see. I wish I could jump in myself.'

'It wouldn't do,' Judith said. 'These small boys, yes. But an elderly gentleman, no. It might bring a blush to the cheek of the young persons.'

There were perhaps as many as a dozen boys, all told, swimming, and fooling around in the grass. Several of them, as Mr Scrape had forecast, were quite naked. The young persons, two little girls of perhaps eight and nine, had sat down on a bank hard by. They were in what could only be called party frocks, but these were of a plain and expensive sort which at once distinguished their wearers from the exuberantly befrilled and beribboned juveniles on the other side of the lake. Here – a discerning eye could at once determine – were either the Misses Barford or the Misses Lethbridge. They sat round-eyed before the unholy spectacle presented to them.

The small boys were far from unaware of their audience – being prompted by it, indeed, to sudden guffaws and random apostrophes, weird caperings, irresolute advances and panic-stricken retreats.

'Dear me!' There was perplexity and even dismay in Mr Scrape's voice. 'Sandra and Stephanie, the Barfords' delightful daughters. I wonder how they can have got here? I hardly think their mother – '

'Pee,' said a small boy's voice from somewhere in Mr Scrape's rear.

'Po,' said another voice.

'Bum,' said a third voice. This time the speaker was planted most impudently straight in front of Mr Scrape's nose.

'Bum!' yelled several of the children together. 'Pee, po, BUM!'

'Belly, bottom, *drawers!*' It was from some child safely up to his neck in the lake that this contribution to the amenities of the occasion came. Complete pandemonium had broken out. Sandra and Stephanie (surely well brought up girls, whom one might have expected to be much displeased) listened entranced.

'Drawers!' repeated a new voice. 'Take yer drawers off!'

There was a sudden awed silence. This was going a little too far. Mr Scrape saw his chance, and grabbed the offender.

'Richard Cyphus,' he said sternly, 'be sure that Mr Pinn shall be told of this. And I shall recommend that you be visited with condign chastisement.'

'You leggo of me.' Richard Cyphus, although at least the spirit of this threat must have been intelligible to him, was undaunted. He squirmed out of Mr Scrape's grasp – not a difficult feat, since he was naked and slippery. 'I'll tell my dad on you. You're nothing to him, you aren't. The ol' blackbeetle, 'e calls you.' Master Cyphus paused, apparently seeking for some ultimate insult. ' 'Ow's yer mother orf for dripping?' he asked.

This brilliant defeat of authority would certainly have produced anarchy once more had there not been a diversion at the edge of the lake. A slithering and panting body had appeared there, and was now scrambling out with difficulty. It was another boy, perhaps slightly older than the rest. Although winded, he was contriving to exhibit a precocious command of words much more improper to be heard on childish lips than any that had been uttered so far.

For a moment something about this apparition was wholly perplexing. At a first glance Appleby had taken him for a young Negro – which would be a slightly unexpected but by no means impossible phenomenon in a remote English countryside. At the same time he bore a curiously mottled appearance – to be accounted for, in terms of this conjecture, only by supposing him the victim of some atrocious tropical disease. Moreover his pigmentation seemed to be dripping from him as he moved. So Appleby's next conjecture was less dramatic. Here was simply a boy who had dived rashly into water of undetermined depth, and been fortunate to succeed in extricating himself from several feet of mud.

But this conjecture was wrong too. What the boy was coated in was oil. And this fact demonstrated itself in a simple and disastrous way. For the boy who stumbled up the bank was in a panic. He didn't like what had happened, and he didn't like the sensation of what was still sticking to his skin. Much as the sagacious Rasselas might have done in a similar situation, he violently shook himself. Appleby and Judith – both rather alert persons, swift in evasive action – escaped the consequence. But both the Reverend Mr Scrape and the delightful Misses Barford were bespattered all over. Mr Scrape – who appeared to be a man capable of considerable self-control in a crisis – produced no more than a vexed exclamation, perfectly congruous with his cloth. But Sandra and Stephanie, seeing the ruin that had befallen their pretty frocks (which they had been convinced the common little boys – who couldn't even afford clothes at all – must have been admiring greatly), set up a concerted howling. And what the wrath of Mr Scrape had failed to effect, this unnerving display brought about at once. The bathers, including the oil-covered one, snatched up any possessions they had, and ran away as fast as they could.

9

'Just what does one require,' Appleby asked, 'to conduct simple diving operations?' He and Judith had shed Mr Scrape (who had hurried off to the vicarage in search of unsullied garments before repairing to his final Bingo session) and were continuing their walk round the lake. 'And I wonder what they keep in that boat-house? Something with an outboard motor, do you suppose?'

'I'd hardly think so. People do keep such things on stretches of water no larger than this. But I don't believe Allington would. Of course, he has a mile or two of river as well, and perhaps he employs a lazy water-bailiff. Let's go and peer in.'

They peered into the boat-house. It sheltered a dinghy and two light canoes.

'Nothing to spew out oil here,' Appleby said. 'You notice that they don't keep punts. A lot of the lake must be quite deep.'

'It's certainly odd about the oil. What can that unfortunate boy have done?'

'He was trying a little under-water swimming, I'd say, and had the bad luck to surface through a substantial slick of it. The stuff may have travelled some distance. There's a perceptible flow of water through the lake.'

'I don't see that diving operations can have anything to do with it.'

'Quite probably not. It just came into my head that some divers have air pumped down to them. And a pump requires an engine. You'd agree that a substantial appearance of oil-pollution in a well-ordered place like this requires accounting for? Let's walk on. The stream flows into the lake beneath the bridge on the high road, doesn't it? We can probably get down there, and back on the other side, before making our final appearance up at the house.'

'Very well. But I can't see why anybody should want to start diving in so unlikely – ' Judith broke off. 'Do you know,' she said, 'Mr Allington and I were having some rather futile chatter about that supposed Royalist treasure. And I started the notion that it hadn't been buried at all, but just sunk in the lake.'

'Possibly somebody else has been visited by the same deep thought.' Appleby walked for a minute in silence. 'I can't think why this is bothering me,' he said suddenly. 'Perhaps it's because of last night's affair having turned out a kind of mare's nest. And here is what you might call a mini-mystery.'

'I think I know who would be likely to leave a nasty mess in a gentleman's ornamental water.' Judith had announced this after some thought. 'Nothing to do with treasure-seekers, or anything romantic of that kind. The *son et lumière* people.'

'Why them?'

'Well, there must have been quite a crowd of them, for a start. Think of the scaffolding. That's it! You know the kind of young men who scramble about on such things – long-haired weirdies, who run dreadful old cars and lethal motorbikes? They'd be just the sort to empty a sump or something – isn't that the word? – into a decent lake.'

'What ghastly class-prejudice! As a matter of fact, the cowboys – which is what these young men are called – are a kind of élite. An aristocracy, indeed, with a terrific sense of style.'

'I don't like their style.'

'Perhaps not, but it's there. And they'd make plenty of row, but they wouldn't make a mess. Spend your working life on a few bits of metal tubing two-hundred feet up, and it will become second nature to you not to dump anything in the wrong place. Bad psychology, Judith. Try again.'

'It's not me who's bothered by a patch of oil. So try yourself.'

Appleby didn't try. When Judith took on her air of having emerged triumphantly from an argument he frequently had recourse to meditative silence. Moreover they had come to quite a stiff climb, for the path they were following had left the margin of the lake and was ascending to a cliff-like promontory set boldly above it. They paused on the summit, and within the shade of a small ruined tower. It was a tower which had never been other than a ruin, and Judith laughed as she walked round it.

'Repton again, I suppose,' she said. 'Or perhaps an earlier practitioner of the same sort. Think of bothering to put up a fake like this when you had a genuine medieval castle half-a-mile away.'

'And perched on the edge of a little precipice which has been manufactured at the same time, I think.' Appleby walked to the edge. 'First a mini-mystery, and then a mini-precipice.'

'What would happen if you fell straight into the water from here?'

'You would inevitably get very wet, and you might or might not be killed. Look! People are starting to leave the fête, loaded with their spoils. But there are a few latecomers arriving as well.'

They looked across the lake. There were pedestrians on the long drive, and a few cars nosing cautiously past them and past each other; those arriving were mirrored in the clear water with a curiously toy-like effect. Nearer the house the ice-cream van had appeared, perhaps having finally sold out to Richard Cyphus and his deplorable associates. Only the faintest noise came over the water. From this distance, the entertainment at Allington might have been a private garden party of the most decorous sort.

Perhaps from a sense that they were playing truant, the Applebys moved rapidly downhill again. But at a point where the path took a sharp turn, Judith halted suddenly.

'A spy!' she said.

It was, of course, a needlessly dramatic exclamation. Still, the facts could be interpreted that way. Straight in front of them, somebody was crouched behind a bush, scanning the surface of the lake with binoculars.

It was a young man. This was plain, because he had risen and faced them. He had been thus prompted – it was embarrassingly evident – as a result of hearing precisely what Judith had said. Fortunately, he seemed unoffended, and indisposed to be at all at a loss.

'Hullo,' the young man said cheerfully. 'Are you bird-watching too?'

The Applebys disclaimed this as their present concern, while at the same time indicating interest in, and approbation of, the pursuit in a general way.

'Then I don't suppose you'll have seen any great grey-shrikes? They're what I'm out for.'

'No, we haven't,' Judith said, and eyed the young man curiously. 'And aren't you a little confused? The great grey-shrike's an autumn and winter visitor. I'd be very surprised to see one before September. And then probably it would be on the east coast. Perhaps you mean the red-backed-shrike?'

'Yes, that's it – or, rather, no.' The young man appeared to suspect a trap. 'I'm a beginner, as a matter of fact.'

'The red-backed-shrike is the butcher-bird. And would be quite in order. It's here in summer, all over south and central England.'

'Is that so – the butcher-bird? Jolly interesting!' The young man was stuffing his binoculars into their leather case, rather as if meditating flight. 'I'm keen on trees, too,' he said. 'Rather better on trees, as a matter of fact. By the way, I hope you don't think I'm trespassing.'

'We've no title to,' Appleby said. 'We're merely the guests of the owner for the afternoon – at half-a-crown a head.'

'At half-a-crown – ?' The young man broke off. 'Oh, of course. The fête. Did you see the *son et lumière*?'

'No, neither of us saw that.'

'A pity.' The young man seemed dashed. 'But about my not being exactly a trespasser. Have you met George Barford?'

'We've met Sandra and Stephanie – in a fashion. Perhaps George is their father? If so, we're to meet him later.'

'I see.' The young man appeared to take note of this indication of the standing of the Applebys. 'Well, George Barford – who's married, you know, to a niece of Mr Allington – is a kind of cousin of mine. As a matter of fact, it was he who got me the job.'

'As Allington's accredited bird-watcher?' Judith asked. 'If so, it was a rash appointment.'

'Of course not.' The young man appeared decently confused. 'Writing the script for the *son et lumière*. My name's Tristram Travis. I'm a historian of sorts, and I come from Oxford.'

The Applebys introduced themselves.

'But I still haven't explained,' Mr Travis said cheerfully. 'Of course that was all rot about the birds. Do you happen to know a lady called Mrs Junkin?'

'Yes,' Judith said. 'She makes meringues.'

'That's right. And she has an astoundingly beautiful granddaughter. Mavis. Mavis Junkin. A marvellous name.' Mr Travis, who was a good-looking youth, gazed with the largest candour at Judith. 'I'm madly in love with her. My only object in being here is to catch a glimpse of her. Through these.' Mr Travis tapped the binocular-case.

'Do you mean,' Appleby asked, 'that you have the unfortunate temperament of a *voyeur*, and can achieve romantic ecstasy only at a remove and through a pair of field-glasses?' It would clearly be a great mistake, he was thinking, to believe anything that Tristram Travis said.

'Not that at all. Mrs Junkin, who belongs to the virtuous poor, has banished me from her granddaughter's sight. I've been unable to persuade her that my intentions are honourable. It's terribly unfair. Lady Appleby – I think it is Lady Appleby? – will you help me in my suit?'

'Certainly not. But I shall look forward to seeing the ravishing Miss Junkin. And now, I think we must walk on. We have to put in an appearance again at the Park before going home. Are you banished from the entire district, Mr Tristram? Does Mr Allington support Mavis' grandmother?'

'I don't think he'd mind my calling. As a matter of fact, we got on quite well. Over the *son et lumière*, that is. I stayed at Allington, you see, to do the research. That's how I met Muriel.'

'Mavis.'

'That's right – Mavis. I wonder if I might come along with you? Would you mind? I have quite good manners.'

'And morals to match.' Judith laughed – causing her husband to conclude gloomily that she had taken a fancy to this idiotic young man. Not, probably, that he was all that idiotic. He was simply putting on a turn – and the point of the joke seemed to be that nobody was expected to be taken in by it. Which was excessively foolish in itself. And this meant that one's view of Mr Travis appeared to move rapidly in a closed circle. Appleby decided to exercise the privilege of an elderly man and ask some direct questions.

'Of course you can come along with us,' he said. 'You read History at Oxford?'

'Thank you so much. Read History? Yes, I did.'

'And took a First Class in the School?'

'Yes.'

'So that you are now a junior fellow of a college, or at least on the way to being that?'

'Yes.' Travis looked demurely at Appleby. 'I'm afraid that to a person like yourself it must all be terribly obscure. Will there be drinks at the Park, do you think?'

'Champagne,' Judith said. 'It's to celebrate the close of an unusually hectic period in the quiet Allington year. There's even been a corpse.'

'A corpse, Lady Appleby?' They were now all three moving down towards the lake together. But Mr Travis appeared sufficiently startled to come momentarily to a halt.

'An unfortunate man was found electrocuted among the *son et lumière* stuff last night. By my husband, as a matter of fact.'

'What a queer thing to get out the champagne on top of.' Travis walked on. 'But then this chap Allington, you know, is rather a strange character. I didn't get on his wave-length, at all.'

'I understood you to say,' Appleby interposed, 'that you had enjoyed good relations with him.'

'That's perfectly true. He took the historical basis of his blessed entertainment quite seriously. He wouldn't have hired a chap like me to dig it out and write it up – not if he'd felt any old thing would do. And anything *would* have done, of course. From a historical point of view, it obviously isn't a very critical audience that rolls in its buses into an affair of that sort. By the way, they've left the hell of a mess, haven't they? And the lorries taking away all that hardware, I suppose. Look over there.' Travis suddenly got out his field glasses again, and handed them to Judith. 'Verges chewed up along the drive, and some damage to perfectly decent trees. That big white gate knocked clean off its hinges. Of course you can't have a show like that without a lot of disturbance and quite a bit of damage. The question I kept asking was, why on earth the chap did it.'

They had arrived near the end of the lake, and were looking across its narrowing extremity towards the high road and the entrance to the drive. Allington Park had a grander approach from another quarter, with a beech-avenue which had arisen like everything else, presumably, at Humphrey Repton's command. It was this route that Appleby had come and gone by on the previous night. But it was in some decay, and seemed not much used. The alternative entrance was a modest affair without a lodge, and merely signalised by the gate to which Travis had pointed. Judith looked at it now.

'The gate has merely been lifted clear,' she said. 'But I agree there's rather a mess. You say you're surprised that Mr Allington went in for it all? I gather it made quite a lot for charity.'

'I suppose that was it.' Travis sounded unconvinced. 'Anyway, he had me do my part of the job pretty thoroughly, as I said.'

'A kind of research job?' Appleby asked. 'And here at Allington? I'd hardly have supposed there would be much to examine. The castle was destroyed during the Civil War, and the Allingtons seem to have disappeared –'

'It wasn't quite like that. Some of the Cavalier families, of course, lost estates, and their descendants never recovered them. The then

Lord Allington – Rupert – took himself off to France, and died long before 1660. But there were others around, and one of them did a good deal in the way of collecting family records and so forth. Much later – in the mid-nineteenth century – all that was bought up by the second Mr Osborne, who had antiquarian interests and a desire to possess himself of anything connected with the place. When the last Osborne – '

'Wilfred?' Judith asked.

'Yes. When he sold the Park to Owain Allington, he threw all that stuff in. The contents of what may fairly be called a respectable muniment-room. That's what I had the run of, and it was quite interesting. Not that there was really a great deal that helped with the *son et lumière*. That had to be an affair, as you can guess, of pretty broad effects. I think the doddering old Wilfred – '

'Mr Osborne,' Judith said, 'is a very old friend of mine.'

'Oh, I see. I'm sorry.' Mr Travis was not distinguishably abashed. 'What I was going to say was that it was very decent of him to let the Allington records go with the place. It can only have been because an Allington – and in the direct line from Rupert, you know – was taking over again. Showed a nice feeling, all the same.'

'What about that treasure?' Appleby asked abruptly.

'Treasure, Sir John?'

'There's a tradition, or legend, of buried treasure, and Allington tells me you made quite a thing of it in your script.'

'Oh, yes – of course. People like that sort of thing. Awful rot, needless to say.'

'So Allington seems to feel. Still, you didn't actually make it up. I mean, it's there?'

'There?' Travis stared blankly at Appleby.

'In the records, I mean. You came on material about the treasure when working in this muniment-room?'

'Good Lord, no!' Travis was amused. 'I haven't at all traced the story to its origin. It exists in the county histories, and local antiquarian books. I wrote it in from stuff like that. I didn't at all go after its provenance.'

'You disappoint me.' Appleby smiled amiably at Tristram Travis. 'I'd have expected more curiosity in a rising young Oxford scholar. But one forgets, of course. You were being a good deal distracted.'

'Distracted?'

'A fickle swain,' Appleby said to Judith. 'The beautiful Mavis Junkin has passed from your young friend's mind.'

'Oh, I say! I call that jolly unfair.' Injury and reproach positively vibrated in the voice of the ingenuous Mr Travis.

'You're a complete young humbug,' Appleby said – cheerfully and inoffensively. 'Now let's go and find that drink.'

10

Owain Allington peered cautiously out of one of the long windows of his drawing-room. There was still a good deal of activity to be seen. Those who remain grimly through the tail-end of sales in the hope of bargain prices at the last were plentifully in evidence. One or two old women, hardened characters, even carried completely empty baskets still. The Reverend Mr Scrape, who was continuing conscientiously to frequent the humbler of his flock, could be glimpsed in negotiation over a jar of pickled onions. (The beans in their bottle had been counted; the draw for the gin, lemon squash, tomato ketchup and whatever had taken place; Owain Allington Esquire had been weighed.)

'That's right, Enzo.' Allington had turned back into the room, and was nodding to the Italian youth who appeared to be on his promotion as butler at the Park. Enzo had begun to pour champagne. 'A haven of peace in the midst of turmoil,' Allington continued to his guests in general. He glanced at Wilfred Osborne. '*Pax in bello*, eh?'

The effect of this speech was surprising – or at least it surprised Appleby, who happened to be watching. For Osborne – a benign elderly presence, although not, as Travis had called him, exactly doddering – had flushed darkly, and turned away with some curt word. It was necessary to suppose that a joke had been intended, and that it had decidedly failed to come off.

'Judith,' Appleby murmured to his wife, 'what on earth was that about?'

'It was about the motto of the Duke of Leeds.' Judith had secured one of the first glasses of champagne.

'I don't see why that should nettle Wilfred.'

'Osborne was the family name of the Leedses. And the first Mr Osborne – *our* first Mr Osborne, I mean, who imported all that tallow – pinched the Leeds arms and motto. Not that he mayn't have been a relation. The dukes were descended from a London merchant.'

'I see.' It was one of the occasions upon which Appleby marvelled at the amount of useless information of this kind that Judith stored in her head. 'Well, I suppose it was a tactless quip of Allington's. This was Wilfred's own drawing-room only a few years ago, after all.'

'A man isn't well-bred just because he's descended from some jumped-up fellow in the reign of Henry the Eighth.'

'Oh, isn't he? I didn't know.' Appleby, who had also got hold of a glass of champagne, made rather a rapid business of drinking it. 'Then don't you think,' he said hopefully, 'that Wilfred might like to be taken away now? Perhaps he doesn't like any of these people very much. I'm pretty sure I don't.'

'I like Enzo. He's extremely handsome.'

'Judith, I do not propose to remain here simply in order that you may initiate an amour with a menial. It's worse than that fellow Travis and his Miss Junkin.'

'I'd like to do some studies of Enzo. I believe he'd make a lovely bronze. Do you think Mr Allington would lend him to me?'

'He'd put the worst construction possible on anything of the sort. So would Enzo. Let's clear out.'

'We can't possibly. Not for a quarter of an hour.' Judith was firm. 'You've been introduced to these people. You must get round at least half of them.'

'Oh, very well.' Appleby resigned himself to his fate. 'You go clockwise and I'll go anti-clockwise. When we meet, that's it.'

'That's it.'

Appleby's first attempt at communication was with Rasselas. The creature, after all, now bore a familiar face. But Rasselas appeared to disapprove of the party – unreasonably, since all the guests were persons of some consideration in the neighbourhood. And even towards Appleby, whom he had so recently met upon a more intimate occasion, he now maintained an air of marked reserve. Appleby passed on.

'Sir John Appleby, I think?'

The question – which had been delivered into his left ear – made an extremely agreeable impression at once. This was because the voice uttering it had carried a quite mysteriously attractive quality. He turned, and saw that the voice's owner was a dazzlingly pretty girl.

'I'm Hope Allington, a niece of Owain's. I arrived rather late. I think you've met my sisters and their husbands.'

'How do you do. Yes, indeed. And their sons and daughters as well.' Appleby realized as he spoke that Hope Allington was a great surprise to him. He must have formed a picture of her at the moment when her uncle had made his silly joke about Hope still hoping. She was at least fifteen years younger than either of her sisters. And all the hoping in her neighbourhood must surely be on the part of blindly adoring young men.

'I approve of hospitality,' Hope Allington was saying. 'But I do find myself doing sums in my head. Here are all my uncle's nicest friends – including now, I'm so glad to think, Lady Appleby and yourself. And you have all, ever so gallantly, rallied round the dear old Vicar and his jumble sale – '

'I don't think it has been *exactly* a jumble sale. As a technical term – '

'I'm sure you're right.' Miss Allington raised her voice, and her glass at the same time. 'So we all have champagne.' Abruptly, she lowered it again. 'What some of these people call champers. Don't you think that's awful?'

'It seems to me scarcely outside the boundaries of permissible jocularity.' Appleby marked, with inward gloom, the manner in which, nowadays, he turned out this elderly sort of wit. 'But what are the sums?'

'The cost of the champagne, as compared with the takings on the jellies and jams out there in the park.'

'You forget Mr Scrape's Bingo. That must bump up the takings. And I imagine that a great deal of pleasure is given by such an affair, even if not all that money is received. Mrs Junkin goes home all aglow from praise of her meringues. Mr Goodcoal feels that the very latest in electronic science has been lavished on us. Such imponderables, Miss Allington, must not be missed out of the account.' Appleby smiled urbanely at the young person before him. She deserved to be called absolutely beautiful. Which didn't mean that what he was himself thinking of wasn't what Judith would have provided for dinner. No more, alas, he told himself, the heyday in the blood.

'Can you tell me who the young man is, standing rather awkwardly in the corner?' Hope gestured almost imperceptibly with her champagne glass. 'I mean the one who doesn't know what to do with his large feet.'

'His name is Tristram Travis. He helped your uncle with the *son et lumière*.'

'Yes, of course. How stupid of me. I have met him. But don't you think he looks as if he had barged in?'

'He has.'

'Then I suppose I ought to go and talk to him kindly.' Miss Allington seemed in no hurry to do this. 'I think he comes from Oxford. They're usually a bit awful, don't you think?'

'Perhaps you prefer the less sophisticated classes.' Appleby gestured away the offer of a further glass of champagne. 'Your uncle's young man-servant, for instance. What do you think of him?'

'Enzo? Isn't he glorious? I adore him. And it's not just his being handsome. I think he's almost perfectly made.'

'I see. May I ask, Miss Allington, whether you are a sculptor?'

'Oh, no! I'm an actress – or trying to be.'

'I ask because my wife is a sculptor, and appears to have formed the same impression as yourself.'

'I see that Lady Appleby is quite surrounded, but I very much hope to meet her later.' Hope Allington, although she talked absurdly and elicited deplorably absurd talk in reply, said this with rapid social competence. 'And now – do you know? – I think I really will go and take compassion on that awkward youth. Bevis, did you say?'

'Travis. Don't be surprised, by the way, if he gets your name wrong too.'

'My name?'

'Mr Travis may call you Mavis, or even Muriel.'

'I should regard that as entirely strange, Sir John.'

Miss Hope Allington turned away. She was very young, but she was well practised in holding her champagne glass close to her right shoulder while employing her left to make a way through the crush. For a moment Appleby looked after her thoughtfully. He wondered why on earth she and young Mr Travis should conduct a love affair – for that was surely it – amid such elaborate subterfuge. That Travis was already married was one prosaic and rather squalid possibility. But if he was, it certainly wasn't to the granddaughter of Mrs Junkin.

Appleby continued on his anti-clockwise course.

And presently it struck him that he was looking for someone. He was looking for the nephew whose arrival the Reverend Mr Scrape had spoken of as almost a solemn event. Martin Allington, the heir of Allington – whom Appleby had last seen struggling for his life against a self-inflicted wound, and before a background of goodness-knew-what: espionage, treachery, blackmail, murder. Rather strangely, he wanted to see Martin Allington again.

This was in his mind when he ran into the Barfords, the parents of Sandra and Stephanie. George Barford was some sort of business man, and played golf. His wife Faith – so far as Appleby had been able to determine in a first conversational sally – just played golf. And just playing golf seemed to be the destiny of their daughters, whose schooling they now began to discuss strictly from this point of view. Did Appleby know of any suitably superior girls' boarding-school at which golf was made the chief thing? Appleby didn't. He had some vague information about comparative ratings in point of hockey, lacrosse, tennis. But he didn't happen to know of a school where the girls played golf all day. The eyes of George and Faith Barford began to stray away from Appleby in search of potentially more interesting company. And Appleby had produced a final meaningless murmur preparatory to moving on when it occurred to him that the Barfords might have information about their kinsman.

'Do you happen to know,' he asked, 'whether Martin Allington has arrived yet?'

Mr Barford's response to this was surprising; it consisted of a kind of short, savage bark which for a moment caused Appleby to look round for Rasselas. But Rasselas, of course, could be relied upon not to make such noises in company. The topic of golf does not particularly lend itself to savage ejaculation, and so far Appleby had failed to remark that George Barford was a man of vehement nature. But this now clearly appeared. The mention of his wife's brother (which was presumably what Martin Allington was) had produced what could only be called a ferocious response.

'Martin isn't here yet,' Faith Barford said. She was looking at her husband rather apprehensively, much as if he were a golf-ball in a definitely difficult lie.

'Broken his rotten neck, perhaps,' Barford said. 'And a damned good – '

'George, dear, there are Colonel and Mrs Pride. I believe they have a daughter of just Sandra's age. We positively must speak to them.' And Mrs Barford led her explosive husband away. She didn't appear by nature to be a woman apt for prompt action – unless, perhaps, in the way of choosing between one approach shot and another. But necessity had constrained her, presumably, to cope with moments like this.

Appleby moved on once more. If he had to talk to people, he would balance up on the Barfords by seeking out the Lethbridges, to whom he had already made a fleeting bow. He thought of it as balancing up presumably because there was a kind of equipollence between these two families. Faith Allington had married George Barford and presented him – during brief absences from the links – with the two daughters, Sandra and Stephanie, who had passed so instructive an afternoon at the bathing-place. Charity Allington had married Ivon Lethbridge, and for long they had been prominent names in the world of lawn tennis – so prominent in mixed doubles, indeed, that it would have been a natural expectation that their marital partnership should produce a girl and a boy. The result, in fact had been Eugene and Digby, identical twins now seemingly about fourteen years old, and at present refreshing themselves in a corner from a number of not quite empty champagne bottles. Sandra and Stephanie were observing this raffishness with awe. They had been shoved into clean frocks. They were certainly having a wonderful afternoon.

'I expect your boys are keen on tennis?' Appleby asked Ivon Lethbridge. He felt that he was beginning to pick up the right conversational tone with Owain Allington's kinsfolk. It wouldn't have been at all the right tone with Owain Allington himself. Perhaps this explained why it was Martin Allington who was to inherit the Park.

'Keen as mustard, the idle little beggars. Can't get them to stop. Can't get them to open a book. School reports positively shocking. Get themselves tanned for negligent work about once a week. They don't give a damn. Tough as they come, the graceless little brutes.'

'Do you coach them yourself?' It didn't seem to Appleby that Lethbridge was exactly dispraising his children.

'Good Lord, no. Have a fellow in for that. Caesar and the geography of South America just now. But they pay no attention to him. Laugh at him. I ought to tan them myself.'

'I didn't mean that. Do you coach them at their tennis?'

'Heavens, yes, Carrie takes the one, and I take the other. Turn about. Six hours a day. It's the only method, you know. And one thing at a time. These hols, it's top-spin. Digby's coming on. But Eugene's going off.'

'That must be very disturbing. Perhaps he should be tanned.'

'No, no.' Ivon Lethbridge rebutted this suggestion seriously. 'It's like dogs, you know. Tap 'em on the nose with a rolled newspaper, but don't lam into them.'

'I see. But Eugene doesn't seem to have much nose to be tapped. Nor Digby, for that matter, since they're alike as two peas. But I'm glad it's all done by kindness.'

'Of course it is.' Appleby was aware of a glance of something like dim suspicion from Lethbridge. 'Latin and geography are one thing. You can whack 'em in with a stick, if you think it worth the effort. But tennis is an altogether more delicate affair. Here's Carrie. Carrie, Sir John is keen to know how to teach kids tennis.'

'Uphill work in our family.' Charity Lethbridge was a large and ruddy woman with a loud and jolly laugh. She was producing this laugh now. To Appleby there came a distinct remembrance that her game had been based on an annihilating first serve, backed at need by ferocious forehand drives. And she certainly didn't seem a woman who made any very subtle approach to things now. 'Ghastly little bookworms,' she said amid further laughter. 'You can hardly drag them on the court.'

'I'm very sorry to hear it.' Lethbridge *père et mère*, it seemed to Appleby, held markedly divergent views on what constituted an excessive addiction to intellectual pursuits. But no dispute now ensued. As with many happy married couples, neither probably paid much attention to what the other said. 'Eugene and Digby,' Appleby went on, 'must be very good companions for their cousins. Sandra and Stephanie also strike me as thoughtful children.'

'That's the egg-head strain in the Allingtons.' Mrs Lethbridge made this announcement amid gusts of laughter, but nevertheless managed to convey that she was now touching upon a sort of hereditary family taint, like epilepsy, or haemophilia, or one of the larger lunacies. 'They used to say that my uncle Owain was a scientific genius – although, of course, he did retire from it. And Martin was always brainy. Do you know my brother Martin? It was what made him so nasty, we always thought.'

'Martin?' It seemed that Ivon Lethbridge had just caught the name. 'Hasn't turned up. Inside, probably.'

'But we *are* inside.' Appleby produced this misunderstanding with the largest innocence. It seemed to be the Allington habit to speak disagreeably about other Allingtons to virtual strangers. Perhaps it was another inherited frailty, like the sporadic outcropping of brains. 'You mean that Martin may be in another room?'

'Quod. Jug. Clink.' This time it was Ivon Lethbridge who laughed – as if there was something wonderfully funny in offering these colloquial terms for a place of incarceration. 'These breath tests. They're going to get chaps like Martin every time.'

'Uncle Owain would have heard by now. Because of going to bail him out.' Mrs Lethbridge positively roared with laughter this time. She seemed to have resented her husband's emulating her in merriment. 'Unless he's calling himself John Smith or William Brown.'

'You can't get away with that nowadays.' Ivon Lethbridge shook his head, and for a moment appeared to meditate a reminiscent and nostalgic note. 'Not if there's a car in the case.' Lethbridge suddenly lowered his voice – or at least produced a token effect of this. And at the same time he winked at Appleby. 'Better a fast woman than a fast car – eh, old boy? It's the old-fashioned pleasures that never let you down.'

Appleby was perhaps more offended at being addressed as 'old boy' than he was by the lubricious and indecorous character of this sentiment. He was also getting tired of hearing about Martin Allington as a drunk – and indeed he was getting tired of Allingtons as a clan. So he said a few words more, and then moved on – having made a polite bow to Mrs Lethbridge and offered Mr Lethbridge a fairly frigid smile.

'Chin-chin,' Lethbridge said cheerfully. He wasn't offended, and Appleby felt rebuked. A decent, vulgar soul, from one of our best public schools, who knew that it is only tennis balls that you tan on a tennis court. Not that it was possible to feel much curiosity about him. Eugene and Digby might be more interesting. Were they, in a secret way, clever boys, in whom was beginning to smoulder an intellectual arrogance, a contempt for the flailing racket, for the flying ball with its everlasting top-spin six hours a day? Or were they untroubled philistines, like Mum and Dad? It would be quite amusing to know. But, just at the moment, tight on flat champagne and showing off to their younger cousins, Eugene and Digby mightn't be at their best. It would be unfair to investigate.

Appleby went in search of Judith, and of Wilfred Osborne. It was his turn to be firm. The party was over. And henceforth there would be only intermittent and rather formal contacts between Dream Manor and Allington Park.

11

As they left Allington, Judith took the wheel.

'Which way?' she asked. 'John, would you like me to take the other drive: the one you came and went by last night?'

'I don't think so. It was pretty bumpy. I'd rather go out as we came in this afternoon, straight down the lake-side. I'm not sure that I wasn't being defective as what you call a man of observation as we drove up.'

Judith made no reply, but turned the car in the direction indicated. Wilfred Osborne was carrying a pair of embroidered carpet-slippers, a random purchase at which he was now looking without confidence.

'An enjoyable afternoon,' he said. 'Pleasant to wander round the old place. And Allington isn't a bad fellow.'

'He's better than some of his relations,' Appleby said.

'Well, of course, they're rather urban souls – those Leatherbreeches and Bartenders, or whatever they're called.' Osborne seemed to have produced these names in honest vagueness, and without derogatory intention. 'As for Martin Allington, we've had no fresh impression of him. He didn't turn up. But all very pleasant, as I say. Nice to see poor old Scrape enjoying himself. Decent chap.'

'Wilfred, are you being quite honest?' Judith exercised some caution in edging past a final band of stragglers from the fête. 'Seeing all these Allingtons, don't you rather feel the incursion of the lion and the lizard?'

'Of the what, my dear?'

> *'They say the Lion and the Lizard keep*
> *The Courts where Jamshyd gloried and drank deep.'*

'Oh that!' Osborne was delighted that his memory now reached out to this learned citation. 'There were Allingtons there long before there were Osbornes, after all.'

'But doesn't that, in fact, make it *more* annoying?'

'I really believe it does.' Osborne's pleasure this time was in being presented with so surprising a piece of psychological penetration. 'When I sold the place, I was at particular pains to make it appear otherwise. And I think I really felt that way at the time. It was a satisfaction that, since I had to sell, the purchaser came from that family. But now – yes, it's perfectly true. I'd prefer an entirely new chap.'

'Who wouldn't talk about *Pax in bello.*'

'Fair enough, my dear. But he meant no harm. Lived all his days among test-tubes and things. And you can't speak out of turn to a test-tube. Lovely light on the lake now.'

'Wilfred' – it seemed to Appleby that Judith was in one of her perverse moods – 'if you knew where that treasure was, would you agree to you and me stealing in one night with dark lanterns and things, and nobbling it?'

'Of course not!' This time, Osborne was really amused. At the same time he peered out, first at the surface of the lake and then up and down the drive, as if suddenly tempted to a very easy way of getting rid of the carpet-slippers. 'I wouldn't mind breaking into the house, you know, and making away with all that Georgian silver, with heaven knows whose crests and arms and mottoes, which one feels Allington has simply picked up in sale-rooms. But the treasure – not that it exists – is another matter. Very much Allington property, that must be. Their wealth poured out for the King, and all that, while the Osbornes were running up and down Cheapside, doing a brisk trade in continental armour for Cromwell's New Model Army. That's what they called it, wasn't it?'

'I think so. But I expect the greater part of the treasure wasn't Allington wealth, at all. It would have been amassed here from all sorts of sources.'

'If it were to turn up, I'd think it ought to go to Owain Allington, all the same.'

'The coroner would have to sit on the stuff first,' Appleby said. 'As he'll have to do on poor Mr Knockdown.'

'John, that reminds me.' Judith was still driving cautiously down the drive. 'Did you tell the Chief Constable – '

'Of course. I named his corpse as Leofranc Knockdown, an electrical enthusiast from out Potton way. Pride was dumbfounded. He clearly thought I'd had computers and things hurried down from Scotland Yard. But he was very decently grateful.'

'And will now be eating out of the hand?'

'Oh, decidedly. He's quite a decent chap, your Tommy Pride.'

'It's astonishing,' Judith said, 'how many quite decent chaps there are in these parts. Wilfred goes in for them quite a lot. And now you.'

'Judith, will you pull up?' Appleby had spoken quite abruptly. 'Get the car on the verge if you can. You won't chew it up more than it has been chewed up already.'

They had been about to emerge on the high road, which ran at right-angles to the drive. The lake, close on their left, was narrowing to the final deep point at which there flowed into it, beneath the road and through a low, unnoticeable bridge, the slow-moving stream by which it was fed. And now they were standing on the brink, staring out over the water. But not staring very far. For what was on view on the surface, perhaps less than fifteen yards away, was a large, darkly iridescent patch of oil. It had the appearance of having broken up some time before, and patches of it could be seen drifting slowly on a diagonal course down and across the lake.

'We were right about the explanation of the oily boy,' Appleby said slowly. 'He bobbed up through one of these. But what do you think is under that big patch now?'

'A fractured pipe of some sort,' Judith suggested.

'Or something entirely natural.' Wilfred Osborne contributed this. 'I believe small pockets of oil can exist in the soil here and there, and that it needn't in the least mean any extensive deposit below. You sometimes see it bubbling up in a sluggish stream, and perhaps take it for marsh gas, or something like that.'

'Not on a scale like this,' Appleby said.

'You're quite right.' Osborne spoke soberly, and after a moment's thought. 'Judith may have guessed correctly about a fractured pipe. But – By God, John! – it's a fractured pipe in a motor vehicle.'

'I'm afraid so. In fact, we're looking at the only visible sign of a nasty accident. And goodness knows when it happened. The oil may have escaped instantly, or only after several days. It's certain that a patch of it would take at least an hour or so to get anywhere near Richard Cyphus and his friends at the bathing-place. One can tell no more than that.'

'It can't have been visible for very long,' Judith said. 'With all this coming and going to the fête, somebody would have been sure to notice it. We'd have noticed it as we arrived.'

'I doubt the certainty of that very much.' Appleby was looking broodingly at the sluggish, and now strangely sinister, patch. 'It's not all that large or noticeable.'

'John, could it have been what that young man – Tristram Travis, I mean – was really looking at through his field glasses? He certainly wasn't honestly after birds.'

'Nor a bird, either – if Miss Junkin may be described as one. But why should Travis be studying this – and keep mum about it? Your mind's hawking after melodrama again.'

'He was scanning this end of the lake. I remember that.'

'And talking about something, or pointing something out.'

'The mess made by the lorries of the *son et lumière* people. And a gate, which he said they had knocked off its hinges. But I didn't think that was right. The gate had just been lifted off, and moved away.'

'To give heavy stuff an easier turn in and out,' Osborne said. 'But it would increase the risk of an accident, with the verge of the lake so near. Deep, too. It's why, long ago, I had that gate hung the way it is. You'll see.'

'Not *in situ*, any longer. But we'll get the idea. Now, just where have they shoved it? It certainly wasn't in its right place when we drove in. I'd have noticed *that*.'

'So you would,' Judith said. 'And there it is.'

The gate had simply been carried off to the other side of the drive, and deposited on the turf a few yards back. Appleby inspected it, inspected the firmly based post from which it commonly hung, and then went back and stared at the water.

'We're not talking sense,' he said abruptly. 'It *isn't* all that dangerous. Who in his senses would have something thoroughly hazardous at one of the two principal entrances to his grounds?'

'John, something *might* have gone in.' Judith was poking around at the edge of the lake. 'Things going up and down have really been going awfully close.'

'My dear girl, that's quite a different matter from clutching your steering-wheel and making a bee-line for the spot where all that oil now is. But I'll grant you one thing. If anybody *had* done that – suicidally, say – the mess here is such that you couldn't easily find the marks of it. Certainly not if it was a little time ago. Before all the heavy stuff being trundled out this morning, for instance.' He turned back to the gate and stared at it. 'Bother the dumb thing!' he said. 'I believe it's trying to tell me something.'

'Perhaps,' Judith said, 'to suggest appropriate action.'

'That, of course.' Appleby shook his head grimly. 'But whatever has happened, a further five minutes is going to make no difference to it now. Has Pride left the Park, did you notice?'

'I don't think so. He and his wife must be about the last people there. Apart from all those relations.'

'Wilfred, do you mind?' Appleby turned to Osborne. 'There's almost certainly something here for the police. The simplest thing will be to go back to the house. And Allington should know at once, too. For let's face it.'

'Face it, my dear John?' There was dismay in Osborne's voice.

'If there's anybody down *there*' – and Appleby pointed into the lake – 'it's a little more likely – wouldn't you say? – to be the missing Martin Allington than anybody else.'

'But why should – '

'He's said to be quite a bit of a drunk, for one thing. It's claimed as something of a factor in motor accidents, from time to time.' Appleby realized he had spoken impatiently. 'I'm sorry, Wilfred. There's something else in my mind, and I just can't lay a finger on it. But I keep on feeling that it's about that gate.'

'We can find out about just who moved it,' Judith said. 'And when, and why.'

'Yes, almost certainly we can do that.' Appleby paused. 'As you know, I never drove into the Park by this route until today. But I've been along this road often enough. And somehow – ' He broke off.

'My dear fellow, it's bound to come back to you.' Osborne offered this consolingly. 'And now, we'd better get this unfortunate news off our chests. Too bad, if there's really been a fatal accident. One yesterday and one today would make a pretty poor show.'

'Quite so,' Appleby said. 'And unfortunately you never can tell when that sort of thing is going to stop.'

PART TWO

TWELVE O'CLOCK AND TWO O'CLOCK

1

Martin Allington seemed not to have changed much – except that, this time, there was to be no struggle back to life again. Resuscitation had been attempted – it always is with the drowned – but from the first it was clear that he had been dead for some time. Probably – or so the police surgeon now declared – he had been dead for many hours.

He hadn't changed. He was the same young man – or almost young man – who had nearly died as the sequel to some discreditable and bungled exploit a few years ago. This time he *had* died. And Appleby, as he glanced at the body for the last time before they finally drew a sheet over it and shoved it in the ambulance, supposed there must have been something discreditable in this exploit too. Nothing criminally so – except, indeed, that it is highly criminal to be driving a powerful car when drunk. And drunk he must have been. No man, when sober, could have produced a miscalculation that would so send his vehicle and himself like a projectile into the lake.

It was true that the steering might have failed at a critical moment. The accident could certainly have been produced by that. Or conceivably a sudden failure of the brakes might have had the same effect, although this seemed less likely. All that would have to be investigated. They had managed to hoist the car out of the lake now, and it was lying on the other side of the drive, with a constable standing guard over it. It was covered in mud and its own oil; it was festooned with duckweed. Otherwise, there didn't seem to be much wrong with it. After it had been poked about in for the coroner's benefit, it might well run again. It was a smart as well as powerful affair: a coupé (which was why the man inside hadn't had a chance) that would look well in a second-hand saleroom. Another proud owner might take that wheel – and never know anything about this small, unfortunate occasion.

Martin Allington would also be poked about in for the coroner's benefit. It happens to anybody who isn't careful to die in a totally explicable manner in his bed. His breath – Appleby told himself – had been challenged for the last time: down there, and as he struggled to free himself beneath six feet of water. But there were other tests. Alcohol would have stopped oxidizing more or less at the moment of death. Or it would break down in a different way and at a different tempo. The coroner would sagely listen to scientific evidence on this. And if anything proved to turn on it – which seemed unlikely – one expert would testify against another. Nothing of which would help the poor devil who had come to this nasty end.

Two deaths by misadventure... Appleby walked slowly up the drive to Allington Park again. Judith was still there, and Wilfred Osborne. It would be necessary to speak further decent words to Owain Allington – who had by now, perhaps, begun to recover from the state of shock into which the first news had plunged him. It might even be necessary to speak again to the Barfords and the Lethbridges, who might conceivably be embarrassed at the memory of the somewhat uncharitable comments they had made upon a kinsman who, as it had turned out, was no longer among the living. But perhaps the Barfords and Lethbridges weren't like that. What did sudden death mean in the context of the golf links and the tennis court? Match point against Martin. Martin's last bunker... These bizarre phrases turned themselves over in Appleby's mind as he walked – which was a sign that something was worrying him.

Two deaths by misadventure... *And two something else...*

The detritus of the fête was all over the place. Ice-cream cartons and toffee papers were chiefly prominent, but there were surprising variations on this simple theme. The bathing-tent which had afforded a sibylline shrine for the prophetic Miss Pyefinch had been taken down, but its decorations had become detached in the process, so that sphinxes' heads, broomsticks, cauldrons, owls, and similar popular symbols of the forbidden and arcane, all in brightly coloured paper, were flapping over the terrace in a dismal manner. Mr Scrape's marquee stood open-ended and untenanted, like a large white whale waiting torpidly for its Jonah. Here and there, children had been sick and unauthorized dogs had relieved themselves. It was probably Rasselas who was most aware of these latter disturbances. It was evident that he took an offended view of them.

The surviving company were clumped in a large glass-sheathed loggia at the south-west corner of the house. It afforded an excellent view of the lake. One might have supposed that everybody felt a morbid reluctance to turn away from the placid, lethal scene. Only Sandra and Stephanie, Digby and Eugene were not visible. Probably they had been sent to bed. Appleby recalled that, after the first pervasive consternation of discovery, a somewhat unrealistic policy of 'keeping it from the children' had been determined upon by the Barford and Lethbridge parents. So the juveniles had doubtless been tucked up early, with approved books to read. Digby had *Bobby Plays for the School* and Eugene had *Bobby Goes to Wimbledon*. Stephanie was reading aloud to Sandra a stirring romance called *Priscilla's Great Round*. Such works of edification certainly existed for the young.

This idle speculation was interrupted by Owain Allington. He came hurriedly along the terrace to intercept Appleby, and led him down a short flight of steps into a small sunken garden with a pool in the middle. It was a depressingly well-groomed place, all immaculate turf in sharp-edged oblongs, with here and there simpering infants cast in lead and perched on low pedestals. Allington drew Appleby to a marble bench.

'Pride has gone away,' he said. 'He felt he must take his wife home. But he's coming back.'

'I see.' Appleby supposed that the Chief Constable must be among Allington's intimate friends, and wished to be with him through his first distress.

'And I'm equally glad you haven't left yourself. I hope Lady Appleby doesn't mind. I've told Enzo there must be something quite simple for everyone at eight o'clock. I hope you and Pride will get together. Two professional views – even highly competent views, as I need hardly say I know them both to be – are better than one. I rely on you both.'

'I hardly think – ' Appleby broke off, mildly astonished. 'You think there is really some element of mystery in your nephew's death?'

'Of course there is! Foul play, Appleby. We can be frank now, I imagine, about where poor Martin's work lay? One needn't, if you like, actually name the branch of Intelligence. But there it was – and you must know, far better than I do, the sort of hazards it can bring. Martin has been murdered. Because he knew something. And I won't rest until the murderer is caught.'

'I can't say that it seems more than a very remote possibility to me.' Appleby was reflecting that too many people appeared to want to take a melodramatic view of events at Allington. 'But, of course, even remote possibilities must be considered.' He had added this rather hastily. It had occurred to him that Owain Allington might be a little off his head. As well as losing a nephew, he had lost an heir. And that side of his having recovered his old family property did appear to have become obsessive with him. If he now believed that in some incredible way Martin and his car could have been shoved bodily into the lake – and his theory seemed to imply this – then he had better be handled pretty gently for a time.

'And I know you're the man to find the truth.' Allington was now speaking in a low voice which enhanced the suggestion of something not quite normal. 'You solved that business last night, when these local people hadn't a clue. A man called Knockdown, Pride says. I'd never heard of him. Mad on electricity. But all that doesn't matter now. That poor devil's neither here or there. It's Martin's death you must work on.'

'If I can help, of course I'll be glad.' Appleby spoke absently. Two deaths by misadventure, he was thinking. And two something else.

But again whatever was hovering in his head eluded him. And he was aware that Allington had got restlessly to his feet again.

'We'll go up,' Allington said. 'You'll want to begin questioning them all.'

'My dear man!' Appleby was dismayed by this fantastic suggestion. And he snatched – not very usefully, he suspected – at a rational argument. 'If you believe your nephew has died within a context of professional espionage, there wouldn't be much point in my – '

'Don't think I'm not aware of the other possibilities, too. Wasn't Martin to be my heir? To have all *this*?' Allington made a sudden, wild gesture. It was alarming, but also farcical, since inadvertently it seemed directed at the overformal little garden and the foolish leaden *putti*. His voice rose a pitch. 'So don't they all hate him?'

And Owain Allington turned and walked away. He stumbled a little as he climbed the small flight of shallow steps again. It was as if, for a moment, he was actually disabled by some access of emotion. Appleby followed him, and they walked in silence to the loggia. Yes, there was no doubt about the emotion. It vibrated in the air. But what really occasioned it, and at what it was truly directed, Appleby didn't think he knew.

The loggia was crammed with that sort of garishly coloured and over-stuffed furniture, much of it elaborately suspended on massive springs, that prosperous persons judge appropriate in such places. The champagne phase of the party having so disastrously concluded, gin had supervened. Several bottles of it, flanked by sundry alternative concomitants, stood on a side-table. Every now and then a Lethbridge or a Barford managed (being of athletic habit) to struggle out of one or another swaying or bucketing contraption to seek further comfort from this source. Wilfred Osborne appeared to have found some tonic water, and also a window ledge on which it was possible to sit in a more or less upright posture. He had his most relaxed and diffidently amiable air – which meant (Appleby felt he now knew) that he was taking a poor view of things. In one corner, and with a franker appearance of having contracted out, Hope

Allington and Mr Tristram Travis conversed together in low tones. It was touching, Appleby thought, that Miss Allington should thus still seem solicitous to put at his ease the young man who had barged in and who didn't know what to do with his feet. Perhaps it was a little surprising that, in the distressing family situation which had arisen, Travis hadn't judged it proper to barge out again. Appleby decided that, if any investigating was going to be done, it might well begin in this quarter. So he went over and addressed Travis.

'I've been wondering,' he said, 'about something you probably have the answer to. Which is the oldest part of the lake? Down here, by the house and castle?'

'I don't think so.' Travis appeared to give the matter some thought. 'In fact, definitely not. The original lake was probably not much more than a pool – a deep pool – up near the present bridge. Miss Allington, do you know?'

'No, Mr Travis, I don't. But that would be my guess. The stream would flow out of the pool just as it flowed in, and wander through what is now the park. Then they built some sort of embankment or dam, and did other bits of fiddling around, and the present lake was the result. I believe that's how ornamental waters were usually created. As at Blenheim, for example.'

'I see.' Appleby changed the subject. 'Your uncle says that Colonel Pride is coming back. It seems to be a relief to him. Your brother's death has been a great shock to him – as it must be to you all.'

'Sir John,' Hope Allington said, 'may Mr Travis get you a drink?'

'Thank you, no.' Appleby felt almost shaken by this steely response to his last remark. 'Your uncle feels that in Martin's death there may be a good deal that should be investigated.'

'That was probably true of Martin's life as well.'

'I say!' Travis broke in. 'I think I ought to be getting along. Been butting in, rather.'

Appleby judged this belated discovery unimpressive. It had sprung, one could almost feel, from a momentary failure of nerve. And this seemed to be Miss Allington's view.

'Stay where you are,' she said curtly, and turned back to Appleby. 'I didn't know my brother very intimately,' she said. 'But at least I knew he was a bad hat. Investigation, as you call it, will produce nothing to his credit. My uncle will do well to leave the memory of the heir of Allington alone.'

It wasn't easy to reply to this – the more so, since Appleby suspected it to be true. He took another good look at Hope. She was young, beautiful, and possessed in particular of so attractive a voice that anything shocking she said sounded more shocking still.

'That about the oldest part of the lake,' she said. 'Was that part of your investigating Martin's death?'

'Miss Allington, I must make it quite clear that I am not investigating Martin's death.' As he said this, Appleby was constrained to wonder fleetingly whether it was true. And this doubt made him bold. 'In my opinion, the only mystery at Allington at present may be a tolerably harmless one.' He turned to Travis. 'It *must* be harmless, or you wouldn't have guyed it so light-heartedly from the first moment we met.'

'I'm very irresponsible,' Travis said. If he had been alarmed, this had subsided. He was quite cheerful again. Indeed, he was more cheerful than, in the circumstances, he ought to have been. Not that Miss Allington, Appleby added to himself, was much disposed to strike the note of family mourning. And what Miss Allington produced now was an exclamation of impatience.

'Tristram is quite useless,' she said.

'I don't think that I agree, Miss Allington. And I think you do well to be dropping the pretence too.'

'What do you mean – dropping the pretence?'

'The pretence that you and Mr Travis aren't as thick as thieves.'

'Thieves, Sir John?' Miss Allington looked coldly at Appleby. 'Isn't that rather an offensive expression?'

'It's a mere colloquialism. The point is that of course he's Tristram to you, and you are Hope to him. And you are up to something together. But, in the light of what has now happened, it just won't do. Mr Travis is a highly intelligent young man. They've been telling him so, I don't doubt, since his private school – so once more won't exactly turn his head. He sees that two unnatural deaths about the place make a change of plan necessary. The whole atmosphere at Allington has changed. Policemen – including Colonel Pride and myself – are on the prowl. You two have been in some sort of conspiracy, but with the feeling that you have plenty of room for manoeuvre. Up to some last moment, no doubt, it could be represented as a mere family joke, if something went wrong about it. Isn't that right?'

'Sir John, you are talking in the most extravagant way. Tristram, isn't that so?'

'Yes, of course.' Travis appeared unconcerned to put much conviction into this. 'Being engaged more or less secretly hardly deserves to be called conspiracy.'

'Why should your engagement to Miss Allington be secret, Mr Travis?'

'I think I'd need notice of that question.'

'That doesn't surprise me, Mr Travis.'

'Besides, you know, impertinent questions ought never to be answered in a hurry. Don't you agree, Sir John?'

'It isn't impertinent, in present circumstances, to try and sort you young people out.' Appleby said this with entire good humour. 'And you both know it. You both know why I asked you which is the oldest part of the lake. The question could have only one possible relevance. I wasn't thinking – was I? – of Martin. It's clearly immaterial whether he has managed to drown himself in old water or new.'

'All right,' Travis said. 'I can see that you know. Hope, can't you?'

'I suppose so.'

'Very well. Sir John, we confess. Hope and I have been keeping our relationship dark as one means of keeping something else dark. We want the treasure.'

'That's a commendably frank way of putting it.'

'Oh, no!' Hope said. 'Not for ourselves, of course. As a surprise for my uncle.'

'And no doubt for your sisters as well.' Appleby allowed himself to glance rather ironically at the youngest of the Allingtons. 'Do you know?' he said. 'I think you're a very odd sort of family.'

'If that's so, it's my uncle's fault. Only Martin has ever been of the slightest interest to him. A blackguard like that!'

'My dear Miss Allington!' It was difficult for Appleby not to feel shocked.

'I know he's dead. But I don't propose to turn pious and charitable about him, all the same. He was to have the whole place – and just to play fast and loose with, at that. My uncle isn't a wealthy man, you know. It was just that somehow he did suddenly make quite a lot of money, and he sunk almost every penny of it in Allington. In order to re-found our ancient line. And to create an elder son. That's what they used to call it, when an up-and-coming bourgeois started buying land and planning to leave everything to a single heir. It has been plain from everything that my uncle Owain has said that my sisters and I were to be entirely out in the cold. You can't be surprised that none of us has managed very much to love Martin.'

'I suppose not.' Appleby glanced curiously at Travis, wondering how he was disposed to receive this not wholly amiable exhibition on the part of his future bride. He could distinguish only that Travis appeared unperturbed. 'Well, the situation has changed, Miss Allington. Martin is your uncle's heir no longer. There's an open field.'

'Just what do you mean, Sir John?' There was a startled note in Hope's voice.

'Your uncle must choose somebody to leave Allington to, I suppose. Unless he directs that it be turned into a cat and dog home. I'm not sure it isn't something like that already.'

'There's Rasselas,' Travis said. 'It might be left to Rasselas. Or jointly to Rasselas and Enzo. But I'm being frivolous again. Let's return to the treasure. You think that Hope and I were going to sneak off with it, and get her a fair share in that way. Would it have been a frightfully immoral plan?'

'It would have been totally against the law, Mr Travis.'

'We might have let Faith and Carrie have a whack. But I suppose that would only be to increase the number of criminals.'

'Not on what you might call a voluntary basis, perhaps. Under constraint, of course, it might be different.' Travis paused, and then gave Appleby a most engaging smile. 'I say, Sir John, what about coming in with us?'

'Tristram, you're a complete fool.' Although Hope Allington said this with emphasis, she didn't really seem to be believing it. She was – Appleby could see – an intense and dangerous person. What fascinated her in Travis was his inability to take anything wholly seriously.

'It's really in that part of the lake?' Appleby asked. 'You came on something in all those documents that gave you a strong pointer to that?'

'Almost a certainty, I'd say. The stream went through the lower ward of the castle, you know. Of course the besiegers had diverted it. But there was a bit of a flood, their dam broke, and the Allingtons managed to get the stuff through their lines in a little boat. Then they sank it in the one deep pool available. It wasn't what they meant to do, but there was some hitch in meeting a waiting wagon, and it seemed their only chance. One finds it hard to believe, but there's a big chance that the treasure is there still. Hope's wretched brother must have gone in pretty well on top of it. When they were fishing him out this evening – him and his flashy car – I was almost afraid that ducats and marks and louis and sovereigns would come up with him.'

'And pieces of eight,' Hope said, 'as in *Treasure Island*.' She spoke, Appleby thought, a little wildly, as if this queer vision of her dead brother dripping gold was a little too much for her. 'Why on earth did Martin take it into his head to go in just *there*?'

'Perhaps he had tumbled to a hint of the truth,' Travis said. 'Perhaps he associated that part of the lake with the treasure. And it had a fascination for him. Acted like a sinister magnet. So, when he was tight – '

Hope Allington stood up abruptly.

'That's about enough,' she said. 'I disliked and despised Martin, and I'll always say so. But we can spare him mere mortuary jokes.'

2

The Chief Constable had been as good as his word. He was back at Allington, and Appleby had glimpsed him during the last few minutes, walking up and down the terrace with his host. Owain Allington was talking vehemently, and it was evident that he was still in an agitated state. Colonel Pride was looking uncomfortable, and as Appleby left Hope and her fiancé – having had decidedly enough of them for the moment – it was to find that Pride too had broken away, and was advancing towards him.

'Appleby, thank goodness you're here still. Come and take a turn outside. This is a confoundedly awkward thing.' Pride was silent until they were out of earshot of anyone else. 'Allington has been spinning me a very queer yarn about this unfortunate nephew of his. Apparently he was in Security – MI5, or something of the sort. Allington says you know about it. Is it true?'

'Quite true.'

'Well, I'm damned! But that would be neither here nor there. Not in itself, I mean. Unfortunately Allington has got it into his head – '

'I know. He's told me. He thinks Martin Allington's death wasn't accidental.'

'He thinks it's something out of a thriller, out of some absurd spy story. Chap must be off his rocker, wouldn't you say? Shock, I suppose. Beastly thing to happen at the bottom of your garden, after all.'

'No doubt. I'm not at all sure that Allington is off his rocker, all the same.'

'Good God, man!' Colonel Pride was staring at Appleby. 'You don't suppose such a thing to be true?'

'That this has been an espionage affair? Not for a moment. And I don't think that Allington is being frank with us. I don't think he's telling us what is really in his head. Pride, do you know this family at all well? They seem an odd lot to me.'

'I meet Allington from time to time – as you will, now that you live down here. The nieces, with their husbands and so forth, I hardly know at all.'

'It seems that Allington had intended his nephew to have the Park and estate, and that he hasn't much else to leave. Martin Allington's sisters were to get nothing – and they haven't been feeling pretty. It seems to me possible that Allington himself has been feeling guilty about it, and has exaggerated in his own mind the hostility and resentment that his known intentions have occasioned. And now he's by way of believing that what we have on our hands this evening is a spot of fratricide. Perhaps that *is* to be off his rocker. It's certainly to have cut adrift from any commonsense view of the situation.'

'Well, I'm blessed!' Colonel Pride was dumbfounded. 'And of course it is. Such things don't happen. Or not among decent people.'

'I don't know that I'd express it quite as strongly as that. But they're certainly unusual among the best families.'

'And you mean to suggest' – for a moment Pride had glanced with a not unfriendly suspicion at Appleby – 'that Allington is talking this nonsense about spies by way of distracting our attention from a crime which he believes to have been committed by one of his relations?'

'I don't know that I'm suggesting it. Call it a possibility which I feel obliged to entertain.'

'But the fellow should simply keep quiet! I haven't shown the slightest disposition to regard the wretched affair as other than an accident. Have you? Have you been putting ideas in his head?'

'On the contrary, Pride, I feel that he has been trying to put ideas in mine. Of course, if he entertains this notion – which I agree is extremely strange – that there has been foul play inside the family, he may feel that some sort of evidence of the thing's being a crime is likely to turn up, and he may be laying a species of false trail in advance.'

'It's quite absurd. The fellow ought to be locked up. Do you think' – Pride was suddenly hopeful – 'we could give him a friendly hint to see his doctor?'

'No, I don't.' For the first time that evening, Appleby felt honestly amused. 'He wouldn't take it at all well.'

'And then there's this business about the chap with the weird name. Knockabout.'

'Knockdown.'

'That's right. Leofranc Knockdown. When Allington hears about him, it's bound to set more bees stirring in his bonnet.'

'Hears about him?' Appleby was at a loss. 'But Allington knows all about that already.'

'Ah!' Colonel Pride said. 'I forgot to tell you.'

The two men had paused on the terrace. A lorry had appeared at the edge of the park below them, and half a dozen men were engaged in striking the marquee and loading it up. They must be working overtime. The last vestiges of the fête were to be got rid of more swiftly than Appleby would have expected. It had been the same, he recalled, with the *son et lumière*. He had rather forgotten about the *son et lumière*. And now here was Pride, with his mysterious talk about Knockdown, seemingly coming back to it.

'You got ahead of us there,' Pride was saying. 'And I was most grateful, as I hope I made clear. But my people have managed a pretty smart follow-up I'm glad to say. When I got home with my wife – she'd had enough of this, and I don't blame her – there was a message waiting for me. This fellow Knockdown is a villain. Was a villain, I ought to say.'

'My friend Mr Goodcoal didn't know that. He seems to think that Knockdown was something of a natural.'

'Low intelligence, certainly. Probably what the quacks call a psychopath. But a villain, all the same. A dangerous criminal, Appleby. Something we don't much go in for, in these parts.'

'I'm sure you don't. And I rather got the impression that Knockdown hadn't, in fact been in these parts very long.'

'Precisely. He boarded, as you told me, with some folk of the name of Clamtree, and it seems he was living on a small allowance. He cashed a money-order at the Potton post-office once a week. Respectable connexions. Not gentry, of course, but prosperous trades-people or the like. Keeping a black sheep out of the way, even at considerable expense. I'm told it's quite a common thing now, even with that class. Like the ne'er-do-well cousin you used to keep in Australia.'

'I've never had cousins of any sort in Australia.'

'*Une façon de parler*, my dear Appleby.' Pride paused, as if taking satisfaction in his command of this cultivated expression. 'Not really a terribly decent thing to do. With this dim-witted Knockdown, that is. Cutting him off from any sort of family support, except for that hard cash. Leaving him idle, too, for the most part. He seems just to have picked up odd jobs here and there. Society at fault, if you ask me.' Pride paused again, this time to mark so liberal a sentiment. 'Still, the fact remains. Knockdown by name and Knockdown by nature.'

'You mean – ?' Appleby was quite impressed by this flight of fancy.

'Violent. A couple of minor convictions. Then mixed up in a pretty ugly gang affair – hi-jacking, I gather – that ended in a killing. He was acquitted. But it was what cooked his goose with his law-abiding relations. Can't think why they didn't get him off to America. He'd have been in his element there, wouldn't you say? But a fish out of water in a quiet spot like this.'

'He tried to interest himself in electricity.'

'The Americans would have interested him in an electric chair. Come to think of it, though, the end result has been about the same.' Colonel Pride frowned. 'Oughtn't to joke about the poor devil. Casualty of our socialist society, eh?'

Appleby accepted this thought with gravity. He didn't feel other than grave all round. Pride's fresh information obscurely disturbed him.

'And you see what I mean,' Pride pursued. 'When Allington gets hold of this – and it can scarcely be withheld from him – it will feed this crack-pot notion of his. He'll bind Knockdown, as a known criminal, into this international conspiracy, or whatever it is. Probably turn him paraplegic.'

'Paranoiac?'

'That sort of thing. Suspecting this and that, all round the clock. Awkward foible in the owner of a place like Allington.'

Appleby didn't demur to the proposition that paranoia is particularly to be deprecated among the landed gentry.

'But all that this fresh light on Knockdown suggests to us,' he said, 'is that Knockdown perhaps didn't meet his death merely as a consequence of being curious about things electrical. He was hoping to make off with some piece of equipment which might be valuable. Nothing more than that.'

'That's the sensible way to look at it, without a doubt. But I'm not sure that you yourself sound very convinced about it.'

'Don't I?' Appleby was a little taken aback. Colonel Pride, he realized, had his brighter moments. 'It certainly isn't that I see any other pattern in the thing.'

'Perhaps,' Pride said, 'it's that you're beginning to feel you want to look for one.'

'I think you may be right.'

'I'll be glad to help you in any way I can.' The Chief Constable appeared conscious that he had uttered this a shade too formally. 'Count on me,' he added. 'I'm uneasy, Appleby, to tell you the truth. It's something in the atmosphere of this damned place. Deuced different from old Wilfred Osborne's time.'

3

Old Wilfred Osborne was making himself agreeable to the Lethbridges. As a young man he had played tennis at some modest county level, and this gave him a kind of toe-hold in the Lethbridge world. So he was offering Ivon and Carrie Lethbridge his views on that year's Wimbledon, with plenty of pauses in which to submit himself courteously to their better grip of the matter. The exchanges had to be conducted in the subdued manner necessarily adopted by those who believe that conversation on general topics remains a social duty even in face of mortality. Not, of course, that Mrs Lethbridge was consistently subdued. Her shattering laugh was so much a mere reflex action that it would certainly have broken out intermittently at a funeral. Wilfred Osborne would wait for it to subside, and then talk gently on. He had such an air of effortless and relaxed amenity of address that it was almost certain – Appleby thought – that the poor old gentleman was inwardly pretty well screaming to be let out.

And that, of course, was what had to be managed. They must get away. This hanging around a miserable fatality simply because Owain Allington seemed to own a morbid reluctance to close up the scene was too silly to be put up with. At one end of the loggia the silent Enzo – Appleby hadn't discovered what English he had, if any – was showing signs of being about to produce the sandwiches which had been commanded of him. Sandwiches, Appleby thought, would be the end. He would choke on the first that was offered to him. Nor was it easy to see why Allington's hospitality had now to be dispensed in this way. Apart from the various members of the family, who had been expected anyway, there wasn't all that of a crowd. It again seemed to come back to Owain Allington and an eccentric notion of what he had on hand. The effect was of one of those comfortless resorts of semi-private theatrical entertainment, more sketchy even on the catering than the artistic side, at which one paces the damp lawns during intervals, gnawing buns and imbibing tepid liquids through straws.

Thus dismally meditating, Appleby looked round for Judith. But Judith, following what was rather a habit of hers, had disappeared. She had probably gone off with a gardener. Or perhaps she had retired into some secluded nook, and was sketching Enzo from memory. So there was nothing to be done at the moment. Or nothing but to give a little morose thought to what all this was about.

Doubloons and pieces of eight. Outside *Treasure Island* and similar, if inferior, fictions large hoards of buried or sunken gold are not really to be looked for. They did exist, perhaps, still all unknown, in what would one day become archaeological sites. They would be unearthed by the sort of people who are interested in Vikings, or in Bronze Age culture. But for anything of the sort stowed away in modern times – and that was certainly where the seventeenth century came in – these islands were really much too tight to have continued to afford a hiding-place. Judith's fantasy of the respectable Humphrey Repton quietly decamping from Allington with the bullion or whatever amassed for King Charles had some sense to it in a general way. Despite the learned young Mr Travis' opinion it seemed to Appleby highly probable that whatever had gone into the lake (if *anything* had gone into the lake) had sooner or later come out again.

Sooner or later. Appleby paused on this. Judith had shoved the supposed recovery of the stuff back to the beginning of the nineteenth century. And one did, somehow, tend to conceive of the treasure either as conceivably *in situ* still or as having been successfully rifled quite a long time ago. But it was possible that it was no longer there now, but that it had been there last week, or a couple of months ago, or only a few years back.

Appleby had got out into the garden, and was at least enjoying solitude. The Allington treasure, he told himself, was so silly an idea that he had now better quit turning it over in his head. But was it? Tristram Travis and Hope Allington, for example. Perhaps they were worth thinking about a little more.

Hope was clever and perhaps quite unscrupulous. Travis went beyond that. He was a thoroughly able young man – and from the first he had put on that curious throw-away turn. What he had managed eventually to put across was the appearance of more or less reluctantly – but still in that ineffective and silly-ass manner – abandoning a project which was still unaccomplished. With the death of Martin Allington – with the death of Martin Allington occurring just where it *had* occurred – it was a project which had become too 'hot' (as criminals were supposed to say) to be persevered with. The matter had been left like that – and with the implication that Sir John Appleby, a benevolent retired policeman, was going to forget about an abortive *coup* which in fact it had been a criminal act to conspire to bring about. That was a fair enough appraisal in itself. If the treasure was really there in the lake, it was no doubt incumbent upon Appleby to take some step for its lawful recovery. Travis had maintained the air of understanding something like *that*; at least of acknowledging that he would not now himself be allowed to get away with it. But he and Hope were not to be chivvied over what had been a mere prank in their heads. Yes, fair enough. But what if, in fact, Travis was being a little cleverer than that? What if this precious young couple had really found and made off with the treasure already?

Appleby had an impulse to tell himself that it would still be no business of his. If it wasn't that this unlikely yarn about a treasure had edged itself into the neighbourhood, so to speak, of two obstinately teasing fatalities, he would have no disposition to give it another thought. The private *mores* of the Allington family were no concern of his.

Yet in this attitude (which would certainly have been censured by a High Court judge) he found that in fact it wasn't at all easy to repose. He ought to have questioned Travis more closely – not that he had the slightest warrant so to do – about the actual documents which had put him in possession of the presumed facts of the case. It had been a circumstantial story: the diverted stream, the broken dam, the hazardous little voyage, the missed rendezvous. How could written evidence of such an episode have survived to the present day without being stumbled upon by somebody and consequent action being taken? It was true that Travis might well be the first trained archivist ever to have mulled over the Allington papers. But records dating from not earlier than the mid-seventeenth century are far from hard going to any reasonably educated man. Wasn't it possible that Hope and her young man had been a little carried away by the natural optimism of youth? What Travis had come upon, wasn't it probable that somebody else had come upon before him? And acted upon – very quietly? A title to ownership in treasure-trove was always a tricky business. In these circumstances, it would be to *anybody's* interest to make no fuss. Anybody, that was to say, prepared a little to ignore the law would be likely simply to secure the stuff privately, and convert it to current coin unobtrusively and at leisure. There would then probably be no point in destroying whatever document had given the original pointer. Its subsequent discovery could do no harm; it might exist in such a context that its removal would leave an odd gap in something.

Allingtons and Osbornes. Allingtons and Osbornes – and then an Allington again. An Osborne had collected Allington records and documents. An Osborne – Wilfred Osborne – had amiably turned them over to Owain Allington with the house. And Owain Allington – for the purpose of concocting a somewhat trivial and apparently vexatious entertainment – had given Tristram Travis the run of them. Anybody who had already irregularly possessed himself of the treasure would not *seem* to be likely to do that. But, if the treasure was already pocketed, what a splendid gesture of innocence!

Suddenly Appleby came to a dead halt. Owain Allington, simply a distinguished scientist, had rather suddenly made rather a lot of money.

But it didn't make sense. Allington's fortune had come to him – one had to presume – *before* he acquired Allington Park. And how could he have known anything about the treasure before that? Might he have been possessed, conceivably, of some secure family tradition, have consequently strained all his resources to gain possession of the place, and recouped himself almost at once by a little appropriate fishing in the lake? Only a lot of investigation could answer these questions. And investigation was something that Appleby had no title to undertake.

And yet – by an odd irony – Allington had been more or less begging him to turn investigator. What he was to investigate, indeed, was something totally different; was a supposedly sinister element in Martin Allington's death. And yet – come to think of it – *not* totally different. There was a tiny link between Martin's death and the treasure. Martin had been drowned at the very spot where the treasure was alleged to lie, or to have lain. The link was totally without meaning on any hypothesis that Appleby could frame. The merest coincidence alone could be involved. Only Appleby, as it happened, had trained himself through a long professional career to distrust coincidence as soon as he became aware of it.

And, of course, there had been another coincidence. Allington Park and its surrounding countryside were quite as peaceful places as even Colonel Pride liked to think. Mysterious events might be described as pretty well unknown. But in the same twenty-four hours – quite conceivably, in the very hour – that Martin Allington had met what must at least be called a rather inexplicable accident another man had died in a tolerably strange fashion. And that other man, the bizarrely named Knockdown, turned out to have a criminal record, and one involving violence. This had to be called a coincidence too.

'My dear John, wouldn't you say that our hour is almost come?' It was Wilfred Osborne who had appeared at Appleby's side. 'And Judith, who has been mysteriously invisible for some time, is now talking to our friend Barford. I should say they have now reached about the seventeenth green. Might we not rescue her?'

'I think we well might.'

'And make our farewells. To some extent one ought to fall in with a fellow's whims, no doubt, when his nephew and heir has just been dragged out of a lake. But there are limits to my mind, and they exclude the necessity of lingering to partake of a cold collation.'

'Sandwiches, I believe.'

'Exactly. And I don't want them. Too much like something or other in *Hamlet*.' Osborne paused in an effort of recollection. 'Wonderful play that. But I'm not at all clear what has put it in my head.'

'Funeral baked meats, I think.' Appleby moved off on the expedition which was to rescue Judith. 'By the way, Wilfred, can you tell me just how Owain Allington made his money? It isn't something that pure scientists often very notably do.'

'He wasn't pure. Or he didn't stay pure. He went into industry.'

'You mean he gave up physics altogether?'

'Oh, no – nothing like that. Of course I don't in the least understand such things. But I gather that he went into the industrial applications of his own advanced research at a very high level. They'd pay him the moon for that, wouldn't they?'

'Something near the moon, perhaps.' Appleby sounded unconvinced. 'But would that really enable him to buy Allington Park?'

'I suppose so. I'll tell you just what he paid, if you like.' Osborne did so. 'A tidy sum, from my point of view, even after the various debts and encumbrances were discharged. But Allington could have earned it, I suppose, if he had something really top-of-the-market to peddle.'

'He could have earned it, conceivably – although it doesn't seem to me likely.' Appleby came suddenly to a halt. 'But he couldn't have *kept* it! I wonder why that didn't occur to me before?'

'But he didn't keep it.' Osborne chuckled innocently. 'He paid most of it over to me. And I live on what was left after I'd settled up the damned bills.'

'I don't mean that.' Appleby had forgotten Judith, now doubtless listening to George Barford getting down a conclusive putt at the eighteenth. He was excited and perplexed. 'Wilfred, do you pay surtax still?'

'Lord, no! Never did – not even when it began at about twopence. When I was keeping the estate going, John, I was lucky if I ended the year with a couple of thousand and my own potatoes. But I don't see – '

'Allington could get some way on borrowed money, no doubt. But if he *was* running along as a professor, or whatever he was, on nothing much, and suddenly *earned* even quite enormous sums, I'd be very surprised to hear he was in a position to buy this estate as a result. Taxation would simply rule it out. That sort of thing can't happen in what Pride calls our socialist society. Only a legacy or inheritance would do it – '

'What about a Nobel Prize – something like that?'

'It would go quite a way.' Appleby was rather surprised by this informed suggestion. 'But I'm pretty sure he has never won anything of the sort. A legacy or inheritance is the only answer – or some really large sum quite irregularly acquired.'

'Some sort of fiddle, as they say?' Wilfred Osborne was alarmed. 'That doesn't mean the Treasury or something could try to get it back from me?'

'It's highly improbable.' Appleby found that he had to laugh at this idea. And then a thought struck him. 'Wilfred, do you mind answering another question? When Allington *did* buy the place, can you remember if the entire purchase price was paid over before he actually gained possession?'

'Good Lord, yes! My legal chaps saw to that. Excellent people. Been going to them for generations. Thoroughly reliable. Not like all those London sharks. Of course I was in their hands, and I couldn't tell you just how Allington raised what was required. But every penny had been paid before he ever entered the place except to inspect it, or as a guest.'

'We'd better move on, or Judith will be handed over to Lethbridge.'

'We mustn't allow that.' Osborne chuckled with gentle malice. 'I've just had him. He's the biggest bore of the lot. And his wife makes the most appalling noises. Laughter, apparently. But I'd keep her in the stables, if she belonged to me.'

'That's a most uncharitable remark.'

'So it is, John.' Osborne seemed genuinely abashed. 'Do you know? I believe there's something about this place now that leads to that sort of thing. Let's get out.'

4

Somebody had hauled down the flag which Owain Allington – perhaps through a mild delusion of grandeur – was accustomed to fly when he was in residence at Allington Park. Appleby wondered whether it would be hoisted again next day at half-mast.

'It's all very curious,' Judith said, as she came up. 'They none of them seem to have cared for Martin Allington at all. And yet – '

'But his uncle cared for him,' Wilfred Osborne interrupted. 'He was going to hand him the poor old place on a plate.'

'You don't sound as if you'd liked the idea, at all, Wilfred.' It was Appleby who said this, and he glanced curiously at the poor old place's former owner.

'You wouldn't expect me to be enthusiastic, my dear John, one way or the other. Certainly I haven't been feeling about it melodramatically. Nothing of that sort.'

'Melodramatically?' Judith asked.

'Well, you know, hoping that each successive heir would drop dead, or anything of that sort.' Osborne produced this strange remark in his most ingenuous manner. 'But, as I was saying, Owain Allington seemed to be able to take his nephew. Doted on him, in fact.'

'I suppose so. At least it's the appearance of the thing.' Judith was looking perplexed. 'And yet I feel unconvinced about it. Mr Allington is upset. In fact, he's in a very emotional state. But I can't quite persuade myself that the emotion is grief.'

They were walking towards their car, and Appleby received this in silence. Judith, he knew, wasn't by way of talking idly in face of affairs like the present.

'And the others,' Judith went on, 'are about as concerned as if Martin had been a poorly trained dog. Yet the household appears to think it would be indecorous to sit down to an ordinary square meal.'

'So Enzo,' Appleby said, 'is furiously cutting scores of sandwiches.'

'Well, not actually Enzo. He's superintending. There are plenty more servants, as you might guess, tucked away behind the scenes. Mostly Italian, too. But they all live out.'

'Judith,' Appleby said to Osborne, 'is tireless in her investigations into how other households run. I can't think why. It's a topic on which she has nothing to learn.'

'The slightest acquaintance with Dream tells one that,' Osborne said. 'So it must be a pure and disinterested desire for knowledge. But, Judith, how have you been coming by it?'

'Oh, I've been talking to Enzo in the butler's pantry. He's on his promotion there since Mr Allington sacked his English butler. He enjoyed talking.'

'Enzo did?' Appleby asked. 'He seemed to me rather taciturn.'

'The poor lad has hardly any English. He welcomed a little Italian conversation. I don't think he would get much of it, somehow, from the Lethbridges and the Barfords.'

'I'd suppose not,' Appleby said dryly. 'Did you gather where he comes from?'

'A place called Pescocalascio on the edge of the Abruzzi. It's rather an awful place. Enzo was quite touched when he discovered I knew it fairly well.'

'He would be. And I suppose you fixed up with him to come and sit for you?'

'Oh, yes – of course. He has promised to come over on his first afternoon off, if I want him.'

'I see.' Appleby, with his hand on the door of the car, stared at Judith. 'Had he anything interesting to say?'

'Moderately, I always like listening to Italians. But I won't bore you with it now.'

Appleby said no more, and they climbed into the car. Judith's last remark had been straight family code. She had something to say that she didn't want even Wilfred Osborne to hear.

This time, Appleby took the wheel, and Osborne sat beside him. On their left, the lake looked particularly harmless in the evening light.

'Do you notice,' Osborne said, 'that this drive looks longer when viewed from this end?' He spoke as if casting about for some neutral topic. 'In Repton's time, people liked what they called consequence. It meant, among other things, trying to make all your possessions look a little larger than they really were. It's not actually all that distance from here to the gate. Shouting distance, you might say.'

'A little more than that,' Judith said from the back.

'Perhaps so. But it looks farther, because of a trick of perspective. As your eye follows the line of the drive, it follows the line of the lake as well. And as the lake is narrower up there than down here, you get an effect of increased distance. It gave Repton the notion of playing a trick with the drive itself, as well. It's a full yard narrower at the other end.'

'Very clever,' Appleby said. 'But one result, I suppose, is the rather tight turn-in by the gate. And it's curious to think what that means. If Repton had been less clever, Martin Allington might be less dead.'

'I wish all roads didn't lead to Martin Allington,' Judith said.

'So do I.' Appleby sounded almost irritated. 'I've had enough of that young man's death as a mystery. And I have a very odd feeling that it's not a mystery and that I *know* it's not a mystery.'

'How very odd!' Osborne said. 'And I'm not sure what you mean. What seems mysterious is the young man's having miscalculated quite as badly as he must have done up there in order to land himself in the water. They talk about his driving when tight. But he'd made a long trip safely enough. The thing happened in the last few hundred yards.'

'Exactly so. And I have an infuriating notion that at the back of my head I know why. And it's a why that would cut out Owain Allington's talk about murder, and Lord knows what. It has something to do with – ' Appleby broke off. 'They're having a field-day,' he said.

Two police cars were parked at the foot of the drive. They had disgorged half a dozen officers in uniform or plain clothes, and a good deal of paraphernalia as well. Out in the road there was a third car, and beside it a couple of men with cameras appeared to be waiting impatiently.

'The press,' Appleby said. 'But they have to hold off until our friend Pride's men have finished their own photographic job. And measuring, of course. That's a good deal more important, and it's what they're up to now. Distances and directions are something. But after all that traffic, the state of the ground's going to tell them nothing at all.'

'That long white gate's still off its hinges,' Osborne said, 'and lying back there where people chucked it. They're using it as a kind of hat-stand.'

This was true. The evening was still warm, and discarded hats, helmets and jackets had been slung on the gate. They were now being investigated by Rasselas. He seemed to disapprove of them.

'Nice dog, that,' Osborne said. 'Well-bred creature. Notice the short, wide skull. Well-trained too. Must ask Allington where he got hold of him.'

The Applebys paid civil attention to these commendations. But Appleby, at least, was more interested in the professional work going forward. Perhaps it was because of this that he made a somewhat absent-minded turn into the road.

'Right, John, you idiot – not left,' Judith called from the back. But she was too late, and the car was already crossing the bridge over the stream by which the lake was fed.

'Sorry,' Appleby said. 'But never mind. I expect I'll be able – ' His words died away, and in the same instant he brought the car abruptly to a halt. 'So that's it,' he said. 'What a ghastly idiot I am! Not just two unnatural deaths. Two white gates as well.'

The second white gate – which stood wide open – was on the same side of the road as the first, and only a few yards beyond the bridge. They climbed from the car and stared at it. And the gate stared back at them – like a yawning, self-evident truth. Standing within it, they were only a couple of dozen feet from the lake straight in front. The track – for it was no more than that – simply turned abruptly to the right and ran off towards a group of farm buildings a couple of hundred yards away.

'I've driven past often enough,' Appleby said. 'No wonder the solution of the idiotic puzzle was somewhere in my head! Wilfred, why on earth didn't you tell me?'

'Tell you, my dear John? I have no idea what you're talking about.'

'Good Lord, man – don't you see? Imagine yourself approaching Allington from the direction in which we came this afternoon. But in darkness. And it's all tolerably familiar to you. You're on the look out for the white gate that marks the drive. Unfortunately it isn't there. It has been taken away.'

'I don't see – '

'So the *first* white gate you come to is the *wrong* one. You swing in, quite fast, believing that in front of you is the straight drive up to the house. But what is actually in front of you is this – the lake at its full depth. And the one gate is so close to the other that a car going in head-on here would land in pretty well the same spot as a car going in slant-wise from the drive. It was all as simple as that. Add that Martin Allington may have been a bit fuddled, if you like. But it could have happened to him while as sober as a judge.'

There was a moment's silence. Wilfred Osborne passed a hand over his forehead. He appeared almost dazed.

'Yes,' he said slowly. 'A much likelier accident. It happened once before. Funny that I didn't remember that.'

'Just how did it happen before?'

'It wasn't exactly the same. There was no intention of going up the drive to the house. It was the end of a long day's hay-making on the home farm. They were still bringing the hay by moonlight. And just as the fellow with the big wain turned in here he must have fallen fast asleep.'

'Horses?' Judith asked.

'Yes, we still employed horses. Perhaps they were asleep too, for the whole thing went into the lake. There was no tragedy. The wain floated, and two splendid fellows I had then managed to cut the traces and save the horses. I had a bit of post-and-rail fence put up. But that was a long time ago. As you can see, it has vanished.'

'Ought we to go up to the edge?' Judith asked. 'Because of tracks, I mean.'

'I think you're right.' Appleby nodded. 'But I much doubt whether there will be a sign that could be called evidence. The ground's baked hard. You can see a bit of a crumble there on the brink. But it might have been caused by anything. It's unlikely they'll detect anything like the tread of the poor chap's tyres.'

'So it can't be called more than a theory of the accident?'

'Probably not – unless the direction in which the car was lying on the bottom has been precisely noted, and affords evidence.' Appleby was looking at his wife in some surprise. 'Call it, if you want to, the more likely of the two possible ways in which the accident came about. But I'd take some persuading that I'm not right.' Appleby paused. 'The question is, what do we do now?'

'Go home to dinner,' Judith said.

'That's the attractive answer, I agree. But I think we ought to go back to the house and explain.'

'I'm against that. We've been back once already. It would be ridiculous. And Wilfred must be extremely tired after this perfectly ghastly day. Our first job is to take him to his house.'

'Very well. But Pride's men, there in the drive, must certainly be told at once. If any faint traces are to be found, they must start looking for them now. I'll walk back and do the job.'

'Very well. At least you're somebody they'll attend to. Wilfred and I will wait.'

'Good. And I'll lay money it's the end of this Martin Allington nonsense.'

'I hope so,' Judith said.

5

Appleby put down the telephone receiver and returned to the breakfast table.

'Smart workers in these parts,' he said approvingly. 'Some obliging forensic characters toiling through the night, if you ask me. And with instructions from Pride to let me have their results at once. Excellent man, Pride.'

'I thought you'd come to approve of Tommy Pride, John. He's awfully like you. I don't mean between the ears.'

'I noticed yesterday a certain similarity in our attire.' Appleby refrained from looking amused. 'Well, they're quite confident. Death took place shortly after midnight the day before yesterday. Martin Allington's, that is. But so, for that matter, they say did Knockdown's.'

'We knew Knockdown was dead before you yourself left the Park. You discovered him.' Judith poured herself a second cup of coffee. 'But now that seems to hold of young Mr Allington's death too.'

'Just so. If I'd left a little earlier, I might have run into him. But no. I came out, as I went in, by the other drive. Incidentally, he had been drinking. But they can't say to what incapacitating extent.'

'And Knockdown?'

'Yes, he'd certainly had a drink or two as well.'

'And so had you, and so had Owain Allington. At that hour, everybody has always been at the bottle.'

'It's deplorably true.' Appleby resumed his breakfast. 'Well,' he resumed presently, 'have you slept on it?'

'Slept on it, John?'

'Don't be tiresome. You said there was something you weren't going to make an ass of yourself about, and you'd chew on it until the morning. The morning has arrived.'

'But, John, there's nothing to discuss. The Martin Allington mystery is a mystery no longer. It has been exploded by Sir John Appleby, and reduced to an accident befalling two horses and a hay-wain.'

'First, there was something about that Italian servant, Enzo. You wouldn't out with it in front of Wilfred Osborne. What was it?'

'The less poor Wilfred's mind is cast into perplexity the better. It was just this. You happened to give me a fairly detailed account of your dinner with Mr Allington, and what followed it. It was difficult to get away. And when it came to final drinks, he fussed because there was no ice. Didn't he pretend to ring for Enzo?'

'He *did* ring for Enzo.' Appleby stared at Judith. 'But no Enzo appeared. We agreed he had gone to bed. And I didn't blame him. It was the devil's own hour.'

'Enzo wasn't in the house at all. Allington had told him that he could go out after serving coffee. And out he went. He's found a girl. The sort you can whistle quietly out of her bedroom and into a field when you want to.'

'Judith, what absolutely fantastic things you find out! And all in half an hour – and in a butler's pantry in which you have absolutely no business to be. But at least we now know that Enzo is a dissolute character. I will not permit his nude presence in your studio.'

'He won't be nude, and if he does come to Dream he won't get beyond the drawing-room. I've decided he's much too good-looking to sculpt. He'd be fit only for Burlington House.'

'Well, that's that.' Appleby paused with a due sobriety over this dire dismissal. 'As for what happened that night, Allington must simply have forgotten he'd told Enzo he could clear out.'

'I suppose so. Had Allington drunk a lot?'

'Quite a lot. And I had drunk quite a lot. We were both entirely sober, all the same. Most elderly men dining together remain entirely sober. Except, conceivably, in the view of a policeman.'

'It was your first visit to the Park, wasn't it?'

'Yes, of course. As you know, I've just met Owain Allington casually, here and there. When he rang up, he asked for you. I suppose he meant to ask both of us for some time ahead. When I said you were still away, he suggested I drop in to dinner by myself. Actually, when I got there he made rather a fuss about it. Hoping I'd forgive such a casual invitation, and saying how much he looked forward to entertaining us both later on. What is called being punctilious, I suppose. He does fuss.'

'Did he give you directions for getting there?'

'Yes, he did. It seemed a bit unnecessary. But it was all part of the anxious-courtesy act, I suppose.'

'He told you to come by the old main avenue, and not by the lake?'

'That's right.' Appleby put down his cup. 'Judith, just what is this in aid of?'

'You see perfectly well what it's in aid of.'

'Yes, I do. You still want to present Allington as a homicidal maniac.'

'I don't think he's a maniac.' Judith paused to light a cigarette. 'But I *am* wondering about those white gates. And all I'm saying is that, if you'd happened to go or come by the lake-drive and not the old avenue, you'd know a bit more about one of them than you now do. Perhaps a vital bit more.'

'I'm taking a little too much for granted?' Appleby asked mildly.

'Something like that. You're supposing, I think, that the gate on the drive was taken off its hinges and put right aside *for* the *son et lumière* – probably when the heavy stuff for it was being brought in – and that it remained like that for some weeks. But what if it wasn't? What if it was removed when the stuff was *brought* to the Park, put back again during the period of the show, and removed again only to get the stuff away? Or perhaps *only* when they were getting the stuff away. That seems to have been a rush job, and it's then that they may have felt they required a little additional space to manoeuvre in.'

'Which would be only yesterday morning, long after Martin Allington was dead. So what may be called my two-gate theory would be nonsense. All this is exceedingly acute in you, Judith.'

'Thank you very much.' Judith glanced at her husband suspiciously. 'John, I believe – '

'Well, yes. Inquiries are being made. I pointed out the importance of the matter to Pride's chief henchman when I walked back to tell him of what I'll still call my discovery. The *son et lumière* people will have been contacted by now. So will the locals who use that road. The result – gate there or not there – may turn out a topic of shockingly conflicting testimony. It's often like that, but we'll hope for the best. Don't tell me, though, after all this, that you haven't got something further in your head.'

'Of course I have. The gate mayn't have been removed in aid of the *son et lumière* at all. It may have been removed in order to bring about what, according to your theory, it *did* bring about: the death of Martin Allington.'

'In other words, poor old Owain Allington went and lugged the thing off its hinges?'

'Oh, not necessarily him at all. Some other maniac.'

'Barford, perhaps – or Lethbridge?'

'They're not maniacs. They're only bores.'

'Hope Allington, then. I'm not sure that she isn't a kind of young Lady Macbeth.'

'Not Hope either. I think I'd put my money on poor Mr Scrape.'

'Scrape?' Perhaps by way of rebuking his wife for this descent into mere frivolity, Appleby reached for *The Times*. 'You would describe Scrape – even outside his Bingo palace – as a maniac?'

'I'm not really quite certain what a maniac is.' Judith seemed perfectly serious. 'But Mr Scrape is certainly as mad as a hatter.'

Mid-morning brought a second telephone-call from the head-quarters of the County Constabulary. The subordinates of the admirable Tommy Pride had been instructed to let Appleby know at once that a thorough examination had now been made of Mr Martin

Allington's car. It was without mechanical defect of any kind. Both brakes and steering, in particular, were in excellent order.

Appleby hung up the receiver, and took a brooding turn round the garden. It was the two-gate theory or nothing, he told himself. And there was a little more to be said for it than he had fired off at Judith. Her notion of the Reverend Mr Scrape or another lifting the first gate from its hinges and tossing it into the grass was absurd. Conceivably two men could do the job, but certainly not one. And Appleby had managed to study the grass in which it lay. He was pretty sure that the grass had *grown* since the gate arrived among it. Dirty work with the gate on the actual day, or night of Martin Allington's death really seemed exceedingly improbable.

But, of course, there was another possibility. Some ill-wisher might simply have *seen* the hazard the missing gate constituted for Martin, *and done nothing about it.* There was something particularly nasty in this thought. It was so nasty, indeed, that Appleby sought briefly to distract his mind from Allington Park by a little conversation with the aged Hoobin. The aged Hoobin, he found, was resolutely opposed to the idea of putting the soft fruit inside cages. Man and boy at Dream, he could remember nothing but nets over the raspberries. It appeared, moreover, that the garden boy regarded such birds as got under the existing nets as a kind of perquisite. They couldn't, indeed, be put in a pie. But the boy enjoyed catching them and wringing their necks.

At the risk of alienating the aged Hoobin, Appleby placed a peremptory interdict upon this sadistic practice. Hoobin turned gloomily to the subject of the moles. Appleby was quite glad when the faint ringing of a telephone-bell called him back to the house.

It was the Constabulary again. A garage-hand twenty miles away on the London road had identified a photograph of Martin Allington. It was an all-night service station, and Allington had filled up with petrol some time between midnight and one o'clock. The man couldn't fix it nearer than that. But he had had a little conversation with his customer, and watched him drive away and negotiate a tricky turn. He had had his pint, all right. But nothing to speak of. You wouldn't swear to his having a totally unimpaired reaction time in a sudden crisis. But he was driving perfectly well… There was as yet no word from the *son et lumière* people, or from anybody else, about that gate.

Appleby resumed his wandering in the garden. He wondered why he was supposed to be bothering about Allington Park. Pride's men were clearly an efficient crowd. They were making all the running. Appleby recalled that he was a retired person, engaged in moving decently from bed-time to bed-time, from lunch to dinner.

Lunch was rather a subdued affair. Judith appeared to have forgotten the whole business. She had brought what she called a *bozzetto* to table with her, and she studied this small wax object with absorbed attention. As soon as the meal was over, she would certainly disappear into her studio for the rest of the day. Appleby tried *The Times* again. He even tried its business section, that last bulwark against the sin of *accidie*. It appeared that a gloomy autumn was likely as car production fell. Feeling out of sympathy with this *Weltanschauung*, he dropped the paper, and stared out of the window.

Enzo was cycling up the drive.

'Your young man appears to have got his half-day very promptly,' Appleby said to Judith. And he looked at her suspiciously. 'Are you quite sure you haven't bribed him to take French leave?'

'Quite sure, as it happens.' Judith studied the young man as he rounded a corner of the house; he appeared to feel that propriety forbad his presenting himself at the front door. 'I'd say he looks agitated – wouldn't you? And I did have a feeling he wanted to say more than he did. It's hard for him, you know, having so little English.'

'I see.' Appleby's suspicion was undiminished. 'Did you happen to tell him that I was a great policeman?'

'*The* great policeman. *Il grande poliziotto.*'

'Good heavens! That means a police-spy.'

'Well, he got the idea, and here he is. We must go and talk to him. Your study will be the most impressive place. Let's lay out some handcuffs. And perhaps a whip or two and some canes.'

'Don't be so exceedingly foolish.' Appleby was not at all sure that he wanted to interview this young Italian – or not under such false pretences as Judith seemed unblushingly to have engineered. But, as there was no help for it, he submitted with a good grace.

Enzo, however improper his nocturnal occasions, appeared a very well-conducted young man by day. He was reluctant to sit down, but did so immediately upon being bidden to do so a second time. Appleby, to whom elderly and morose English upper servants were not congenial, judged him rather attractive. It was perhaps odd that Owain Allington, whose notions appeared conventional, should not employ somebody more like a stage butler. But if the rest of the staff at the Park was Italian, Enzo was no doubt an effective choice for running it. He was intelligent. And, at the moment, he was plainly perturbed. The reason appeared almost at once. The *polizia* had shown him a photograph of the dead man.

It was another instance of Pride's men being on their toes, Appleby thought. Summoning such Italian as he had, he asked Enzo whether he had recognized Mr Martin Allington. But at this the young man was at a loss, and Judith had to clear up the misunderstanding. The photograph had been of *l'altro morto*, the other dead man. And he had recognized the other dead man? Yes, Enzo had recognized him – although he had seen him only once and in the dark. *Prese lungo l'albereto*.

'He was going along the avenue,' Judith said. 'Something like that. Knockdown, apparently. Perhaps –' She broke off. Enzo was now saying something about the *parroco*.

And then, rather slowly and laboriously, Enzo's small story emerged. He had served his employer and the General (who was Appleby) with dinner and with coffee. He had been instructed that he was then free *andare a far una breve passeggiata* in the agreeable summer night. But, for reasons with which he would not trouble the *nobiltà*, he had not set out at once.

'The Applebys are on the up and up,' Appleby said cheerfully. 'But what the young blackguard means is that it was no go until he could be sure the girl's parents were fast asleep.'

'No doubt,' Judith said. 'But let him go on.'

Enzo went on. He had taken the road by the *lago*, and at the foot of it he had come upon a man. It had been impossible to see him clearly, but he had the appearance of pacing up and down while waiting for somebody, and he was smoking a cigarette. He was restless and uneasy, like an animal going round and round its cage. *Attorno attorno*, Enzo said graphically. Enzo, the guardian of Allington, had felt that the intruder must be accosted. Whereupon the intruder had retreated rapidly to the high road. It was still not possible to see much, since the moon had not yet risen. But that was where the *parroco* came in.

There could be no doubt who the *parroco* was. He was the Reverend Mr Scrape. He had appeared on a bicycle – perhaps returning, Enzo said as he crossed himself devoutly, from some sacred occasion. *El viatico*, perhaps. The *parroco* had a very good lamp on his bicycle, and for a moment its beam had fallen full on the face of the prowling man. Enzo had seen the face clearly, and no doubt the *parroco* had seen it clearly too. It was the same face as in the photograph shown to him by the *polizia*. The face of Knockdown. Enzo had then gone on his way. Knockdown was now on the public road, and there was nothing to be done about him.

'He was scared, wasn't he?' Judith asked, when Appleby had returned from seeing the young man out of the house.

'Yes, I suppose he was.'

'Do you think there was something more, that he didn't tell us?'

'I don't know. But probably not.'

'But why should he be so uneasy?'

'He's a long away from Pescocalascio. And perhaps he's another who feels something rum in the atmosphere of that place.'

'Allington?'

Appleby nodded. He had been speaking so absently that Judith realized that the Allington affair had really got John hooked at last. And now he began walking restlessly up and down the room.

'I still want to stick to the second-gate theory,' he said. 'And not any monkeying with Gate One in order to lure that car through Gate Two. It happened as it did through sheer accident. That's the common-sense of the thing.'

'Knockdown.'

'Yes, I know. Knockdown lurking down there, within yards of where Martin Allington was to die. And then Knockdown dead. Damnably oddly dead. But give up the theory of accident – *my* theory of accident, the plausible second-gate theory – and chaos is come again. No sense to be seen in the thing at all. And, for good measure, a really fantastic theme of sunken treasure thrown in. It needs thinking out. What that chap in Baker Street called a two-pipe mystery.'

'Two gates, two pipes.'

'Just so.' Appleby came to a halt by the window, and stared out into the early afternoon. 'At least there's a little time to think about it all. Nothing more will happen today.'

But in this Sir John Appleby was wrong. For everything did.

6

Just before teatime, the second-gate theory was blown sky-high. It was blown sky-high with a devastating simplicity and finality. And it was Pride's men who did the job.

'What do you expect?' Appleby said, when he had once more turned away from the telephone. 'I'm only a superannuated meddler, neither in the thing nor out of it.'

'John, whatever are you talking about?' Judith had seldom seen her husband so ruffled. It was as if his pride were hurt.

'If I'd been in charge, I'd have done just that. Straight away. And saved myself from talking a great deal of nonsense.'

'What would you have done straight away? I didn't hear what they were saying, you know.'

'I'd have walked over to the home farm, and had a word with Allington's manager. That's just what *they* did – rather belatedly, an hour ago. A reliable character with the appropriate name of Mudway, long known and much respected in the district. And he doesn't like my gate.'

'*Your* gate?'

'The second gate. He regards it as dangerous – with the lake dead in front of it like that, and the track turning sharp to the right. Last year, he took down a decayed and inadequate bit of fencing dating from Osborne's time, and he's been meaning to put up something better. Meantime' – Appleby suddenly grinned wryly – 'he closes and padlocks that gate every night.'

'Oh, dear!'

'You may well lament your husband's near senility. If we had come on it half an hour later yesterday, shut and locked it would have been. And shut and locked it was the night before.'

'Well, that's that.'

'Quite so. A most judicious conclusion, Judith. Incidentally, the excellent Mr Mudway remembers the unfortunate affair of the hay-wain, although it was before he was in any authority. He told Pride's people he had no doubt its driver had got tight on cider, and that he wasn't going to have another drunk landing in the lake in the darkness or the dusk. Do you think it theologically tenable that Mr Mudway was Martin Allington's Guardian Angel? He was ensuring that there was at least *one* accident that couldn't befall the poor chap.'

'So where are we now?'

'I can tell you where Pride is. He's swapping, with due compunction, my feasible accident for the much less likely-looking one with which we started. And he's right. There's no other way – '

'Common-sense way.'

'Exactly. There's no other common-sense way of looking at it. Martin wasn't misled by the disappearance of the first gate from its hinges. He turned into the drive, all right, just as he should. Or rather, just as he shouldn't. For he at once took a wild and unaccountable swerve to the right, and did a kind of running dive, car and all, into the lake.'

'Knockdown.'

'Yes, indeed. But just what and how?'

'He was lurking, as we now know. Perhaps with some intention of stealing electrical stuff, or perhaps just curious about it. And we're told now that he'd been drinking.'

'Not a great deal.'

'Well, enough. And he staggered out in front of that rather fast-moving car, just as it turned into the drive – '

'And Martin swerved to avoid him – and that was curtains for Martin.' Appleby paused. 'It's most convincing.' Once more, he began his restless pacing about. 'Only, what happened then? Knockdown was *not* knocked down. He was left on his feet – and treated to the spectacle of a car and its driver disappearing into the lake. What does he do? Potters on unconcernedly to what we called the gazebo, climbs into it, and deftly electrocutes himself.' Abruptly, Appleby came to a halt again. 'It won't do. I give it up. Common-sense, that is. It won't take us through this thing. The true solution is going to be a mad solution. A freakish solution. Think of the treasure.'

'It doesn't seem to me that *you've* been thinking much about the treasure.'

'Perfectly true, in a way. I keep on shoving it out of my head. You see, it leads to something just *too* bad. Martin Allington was diving for it.'

'*Diving for it?*'

'Metaphorically speaking. Madly interpreted. Freakishly regarded. Don't you see? *Why just like that?* He died where he did because the treasure was where it is – or was, or was fabled to be. There! Are you surprised that I try to thrust such insane imaginings out of my mind?'

'Talk of madmen!' Judith had moved to the window. 'There's a very old car coming up the drive. And its occupant is Mr Scrape.'

'I don't know why you should insist that *he's* mad,' Appleby said.

'Perhaps I'm just being freakish.'

'Or why he should take it into his head to call on us. We have our own vicar – and I'm bound to say he's about enough.'

'John, dear, you're getting out of temper. You'll be ever so much better when you've mopped up the Allington mystery – a clear length ahead of Tommy Pride. And now, do go and meet Mr Scrape. He's arrived just in time for tea.'

'They always do,' Appleby said gloomily, and left the room. He composed his features as he did so into a decorous expression of pleasurable surprise.

Mr Scrape had every appearance of merely having strayed inadvertently beyond the boundaries of his own field of pastoral care. Appleby wondered vaguely whether he had, in fact, taken charge of the parish of Long Dream with Linger as a result of some sudden upheaval in diocesan affairs. Or perhaps Mr Scrape was a Rural Dean, with a roving commission in these parts. However this might be, he imbibed tea and emitted clerical chit-chat as if his visit was self-evidently on a regular basis. Along with this, however, he did betray faintly the air of a man biding his time. He had a good deal to say about the kindness of the Applebys in having attended the Allington fête and supported it so generously. Appleby remembered that it hadn't occurred to him to buy a thing. This had certainly been most reprehensible, and he recalled Wilfred Osborne's carpet slippers with proper shame. Perhaps Mr Scrape spoke consciously as an ironist. Perhaps he was presently going to ask for a subscription. It was a little odd that he had said nothing at all about the fatality in the lake. So eventually Appleby said something about it himself.

'Extremely sad,' Mr Scrape said. He had put down his teacup, and it would have been possible to imagine that his stringy form had stiffened. 'So promising a young man, and so beloved by his uncle. A brilliant career cut off. And one who, at Allington, would in the fullness of time inherit so large a potentiality for doing good. We can only bow the head.'

Mr Scrape bowed his head as he spoke, but it proved to be only for the purpose of selecting a piece of fruit-cake. Appleby found himself wondering whether perhaps he really *was* mad. Or mad, at least, in the sense of having a totally unreal vision of people and their qualities. And Mr Scrape wasn't so much parsonical as ultra-parsonical. He was, in fact, a shade unnerving.

'And we must not forget the other unfortunate man,' Mr Scrape said. 'In a sense, indeed, it is for the hapless Knockdown that we should chiefly pray. The circumstances of his death were such that it is to be feared he was among the reprobate.'

Appleby's feeling of alarm grew. If one believed in the doctrine of Reprobation could one with any theological consistency talk about praying for the souls of the dead? Perhaps Mr Scrape led so absorbed a life organizing parish teas – not to speak of Bingo orgies – that he was a little rusty on the theoretical side of his employment.

'The man was known to me,' Mr Scrape said. 'But not, apparently, to Mr Allington. Or so, Lady Appleby, I seem to recall your mentioning. On good authority, I suppose?'

'I gathered it was self-evident.' Judith was surprised. 'John, wasn't that so?'

'Certainly it was. Indeed, Allington has told me he had not so much as heard of him. It seems he hadn't been in these parts for very long. Incidentally, he had a criminal record.'

'A *criminal* record?' For a moment Mr Scrape held his fruit-cake suspended in mid-air. 'You horrify me. Knockdown had performed small tasks for me, and was moderate in the wage he required.'

'Had you employed him recently?' Appleby asked.

'Ah, no. Not, I judge, for several weeks.'

'And you won't have run across him since then?'

'Let me think. No, I have had no conversation with him at all.'

'I don't mean quite that. Did you have as much as a glimpse of him during the past few weeks?'

'Lady Appleby, this is most delicious tea. I shall know where to come in future when the little tea-bell rings. But, my dear Sir John, I beg your pardon! No, I have no clear recollection of catching sight of the man Knockdown recently. But what you say about his criminal past disturbs me. One should invariably require references even from persons whom one takes into the most casual employment.'

'Not,' Judith said, 'that it wouldn't be one who had strayed whom you would naturally be most anxious to help.'

'Precisely. It is what I was saying. But I must go on my way, I fear. I have to call on our schoolmaster, Mr Pinn, to report yesterday's shocking behaviour on the part of Richard Cyphus. Indeed, Lady Appleby, I must apologize for it.'

Judith showed such clear signs of not receiving this well, that Appleby felt it judicious to interpose hastily.

'I hope,' he asked, 'that the proceeds of the fête answered your expectations?'

'I believe they will prove to be such as to be a very great help.' Mr Scrape had got to his feet. 'But there is so much to be done! The upkeep of the chancel is, of course, a charge upon Mr Allington, as patron of the living. I need hardly say that he discharges it most punctiliously. How fortunate I am to have such a man to support me! But the nave must definitely have a new anthracite stove before winter is upon us. And the state of the village hall is, as you know, a grave matter indeed. Moreover, the re-identification of the conventual buildings is imperative.'

'The conventual buildings?' Judith asked. She was entirely at sea.

'My dear Lady Appleby, as one whose family has held property immemorially in an adjoining parish, you must know that Allington was originally an abbey-church.'

'Yes, of course, I have heard that.'

'But just as Oliver Cromwell demolished the greater part of the castle in the seventeenth century, so did his devilish namesake, Thomas, not only dissolve the monastery a century before but actually proved instrumental in tearing the vast fabric asunder. Today, not a stone remains.'

'And you are going to build it again?' Appleby asked.

'Assuredly. It is my inflexible resolution.'

'And re-establish a community of regular clergy?'

'That is as yet undetermined – a detail which will come later.'

'It will be rather a costly undertaking?'

'Not excessively so. I am assured that less than a quarter of a million may suffice. Lady Appleby, thank you for so delicious and timely a refreshment. There is work in the vineyard. An immediate task, indeed. I must take my leave.'

And Mr Scrape departed. His ancient car went backfiring down the drive. The Applebys for some moments eyed each other in silence.

'I did tell you – didn't I?' Judith said presently. 'It's the dynamic behind even his Bingo palace. Mad as a hatter.'

'But it's fantastic! He's the perfect type of the Erastian cleric.'

'Mr Gladstone said that many most respectable persons have been Erastians.'

'Don't be absurd. He's the sort that gets along very happily on the basis of a kind of muddled conflating of the squire and the deity.'

'Perhaps he's what is called a disassociated personality.'

'Perhaps. Anyway, he has some sort of fanaticism bottled up in him. You realize why he came?'

'I don't think I do.'

'It was to make quite sure that Owain Allington had declared himself unacquainted with Knockdown.'

'Why should he want to make sure of that?'

'It could only be for one reason. He knows it to be a lie.'

Appleby spent much of the later afternoon on the telephone. There are some matters on which it is not very easy even for a retired Commissioner of Police to gain information – or not except discreetly in appropriate clubs. He was a shade out of patience by the time the process was concluded, and he was rather pleased when he spied Wilfred Osborne making his way through one of the nearer fields with the evident intention of dropping in at Dream for drinks. Osborne wasn't in a hurry. He had, in fact, paused to hold a short conversation with one of Judith's elderly horses. Appleby had time to go and find a rather more respectable sherry than was lying around. Osborne, although a man of very simple mind, probably had a hereditary knowledge of sherry. If you imported tallow in one generation, you probably imported sherry, port and madeira as a profitable sideline in the next.

Osborne, however, asked for beer. It had been, he pointed out placidly, another uncommonly warm day.

'I haven't noticed it,' Appleby said morosely. 'I can't get Allington out of my head. Did you meet Judith, by the way? She's gone out to palm off some of those jams and pickles on the defenceless poor. She could have taken your carpet slippers as well.'

'I didn't see her. And I thought of giving the slippers to Hoobin, if that's all right. He's one of my oldest acquaintances.'

'Excellent. It may suggest to him that his time for slippered ease has come. He has shown no signs of retiring, so far. And it isn't a thing I'd care to suggest to him.'

'No, of course not. It's even more difficult than with dogs.' Wilfred Osborne shook his head sombrely. '*Fugit hora. Tempus edax rerum.* All that. Wonderful way these old fellows had of putting things.'

'Yes, indeed. *Tempora mutantur, nos et mutamur in illis.*' Appleby paused – by way of agreeing that proper tribute should be paid to Ovid, Virgil, and others. 'Wilfred, how would you have felt, when you sold Allington, if you'd known that the purchaser had just scraped past some shocking scandal? Or perhaps you *did* know?'

'My dear John, I've certainly no notion of what you're talking about. It's possible that I'd have been most upset. I think I've told you that, just at the time, I took some comfort from the fact that the place was going back to an Allington. Old and honourable stock. One gets these feelings, eh? But what sort of scandal? Acting badly by a woman?'

'Nothing like that. They don't call that scandalous nowadays.'

'Perfectly true, my dear fellow. Rotten times. Haven't heard the word cad uttered these twenty years. Nor bounder either. Proves it, wouldn't you say?'

'Certainly it does.' Appleby wasn't concerned with Wilfred Osborne's logical processes. 'But about Owain Allington. You told me how he had gone into industry. It seems he was involved with atomic energy at a pretty high level. And a feeling got around that he was doing a little horse-trading in that line.'

'Good God! You don't mean with the Bolsheviks?'

'No, not that. But with some inquiring gentlemen from the Near East. I suspect his nephew may have been in on it too.'

'They ought to have been put in gaol.'

'We can't be sure of that. There was no evidence of an actual deal. You can at least be tolerably certain that he didn't buy Allington out of the fruits of treason. I've only had this in a rather cautious way over the telephone less than an hour ago. It can't be put stronger than that there were some ugly thoughts going round. And then Allington, so to speak, asked for his cards. That finished the matter.'

'John, this makes me most uneasy. One doesn't want to be uncertain about any neighbour over a thing like that. Let alone –'

'Quite so. But at least you couldn't have had an inkling of the affair when you sold him the Park. You'd never met him, had you, until he turned up as a possible purchaser?'

'Dear me, yes.' Osborne looked surprised. 'Didn't I tell you he was at the Park as a guest? Only two or three times, I suppose. But over a period of a couple of years. He was interested in the family papers. *His* family papers, that is. That's why I eventually turned them over to him. My dear John, are you unwell? Or is it a wasp? Deuced bad this year.'

Appleby had certainly sprung to his feet in an agitated fashion. But he at once sat down again with tolerable composure.

'Where was Allington actually living at that time?' he asked.

'In London, I suppose. But he had rented a weekend cottage in Outreach, and he seemed to spend quite a lot of time there. Carried on some of his researches, you know. Nothing to do with atoms and all that – or not so far as I knew. He explained one of his projects to me. Most interesting, I thought. It was why I lent him the lake.'

This time, Appleby didn't even move. He simply stared at Wilfred Osborne as if that innocent country gentleman had been suddenly transmogrified into a two-headed calf.

'You *lent* Owain Allington the lake? He picked it up and carried it off with him?'

'Let him have the use of it, my dear John.' Osborne sounded mildly reproachful. 'He was perfecting some kind of light-weight diving-kit. I doubt whether he ever came across himself. Just sent a couple of fellows for a day or two. No mess at all. Quite harmless.'

'And I suppose this would have been at the only deep part of the lake – down at the end by the bridge?'

'Quite right. Not that it's all that deep, you know. They didn't need anything of that kind.'

'In fact, Wilfred, this happened just where Martin Allington was drowned a couple of nights ago?'

'Just there.' Wilfred Osborne finished his beer, and stood up to go. 'Coincidence, eh? They're always happening.'

'Wilfred, I think I must tell you – '

But Appleby was interrupted by the ringing of the telephone-bell.

'Appleby – that you?' The disturbed voice was Colonel Pride's. 'Thank the Lord you're in. Look – I'm at this damned place again.'

'Allington?'

'That's what I said. Can you come over? It's the padre. Slope. Scroope.'

'Scrape?'

'Yes – can't you hear me? Get in your car, and come straight across.'

'I have Wilfred Osborne with me.'

'Bring him too. And bring your wife. Be sure to bring your wife. She can talk sense to these damned women.'

'Very well. But just what is this about Scrape?'

'Haven't I just told you? Confound this line! Fellow's been found drowned in the lake. Hit on the head and drowned.'

7

It was dusk when they set out. Whatever the crisis at Allington Park, Judith had judged it not a good idea to arrive there unfed. Appleby spent the short drive in silence. He felt it ought to be possible to step out of the car with the whole matter cleared up in his head. Not that he must jump to conclusions – to any conclusions at all. The second-gate theory had been just such a jump – and it had landed him, so to speak, not in the lake but the ditch. And now the plot had thickened, concentrated itself, in the close vicinity of Gate One.

But the gate itself seemed no longer in the picture. Its removal hadn't misled Martin Allington into overshooting his mark and driving on across the bridge. He had turned into the drive in the normal way. Nor could the gate's new position then have affected the matter – or not, at least, short of some wholly unlikely mental aberration. But, if not the gate, then what?

Cow and Gate, Appleby suddenly said to himself. His children had imbibed a good deal of something called that long ago. So what about the Cow and Gate Mystery? The notion of the unfortunate Knockdown somehow blundering fatally in front of Martin Allington's car didn't much impress him. But why not a cow? A man driving just a little too fast, and driving with just a little too much liquor in him, could easily take some fatally ill-calculated evasive action if a large animal suddenly presented itself in his headlights.

But there was no reason to suppose that any such creature had been around. So the celebrated tenet known to philosophers as Occam's razor must apply. For the purposes of explanation things not known to exist should not, unless it is absolutely necessary, be postulated as existing. This put the Cow and Gate theory – or even the Dog-or-Cat and Gate theory – at least on the shelf. But Leofranc Knockdown (unlikely as he sounded) was known to exist – or at least to have existed. He was existing and on the spot. This applied, too, to the now defunct Mr Scrape, who had turned up so pat on his bicycle. But the young Italian, Enzo, had turned up pat too. Had he told the truth as he knew it? Had he told the whole of the truth as he knew it? Appleby could find no reason to suppose otherwise. Enzo, might, of course, have been in some sinister conspiracy with his employer. For that matter, so might Knockdown – or even Scrape. And it was certainly Owain Allington himself who had most to be thought about. Three men had met unnatural deaths on his property within forty-eight hours – and there was something out of the way in his relationship to at least two of them. With his nephew he had almost certainly been mixed up in the dubious business Appleby had been hearing about in his telephone-calls to London. And it was almost certain that his assertion that he didn't know Knockdown had been detected by Mr Scrape as untrue. Incidentally, Scrape was a liar as well. Or he was a liar unless Enzo was. On Enzo's showing, he could not have failed to recognize Knockdown as he went past on his bicycle on the fatal night.

But Owain Allington was the man to stick to – Owain Allington and his treasure. And the treasure, first of all. The entire mystery, weird as it seemed, really stemmed from that unlikely hoard.

Appleby had first heard of the treasure from Allington himself. Allington had been professing to regret having had the treasure mentioned in the *son et lumière* – this because it had actually brought foolish nocturnal prowlers around the place in the hope of finding it. But had it really done that? It was an unlikely story, when you paused on it. Perhaps Allington had simply wanted some occasion for mentioning the treasure. But why? Well, he'd said nothing about any record of *sunken* treasure. Only *buried* treasure. It was almost – Appleby suddenly thought – as if the fellow was playing a game. And playing it with his new neighbour, Sir John Appleby.

Take the business of the treasure a little further back. There was now a fairly clear picture – and it was a thoroughly astonishing one. The stuff had really existed, there in the lake. Allington had known enough about it, if only as a matter of uncertain family tradition, to prompt him to make Wilfred Osborne's acquaintance, stay as a guest at the Park, get at documents in the muniment-room which could never have been adequately scrutinized before. These had enabled him – one simply had to put it this way – to plant that red cross on the significant spot on the ancient map or chart. Straight boys' adventure-story stuff. But what had succeeded upon it was truly wonderful. Allington had faked an interest in developing diving-kit, been 'lent' the lake for a day or two, and possessed himself of the treasure as a result. It had been a fantastic subterfuge, which could have seemed feasible only as the result of an accurate assessment of the honourable simplicity of Wilfred Osborne's mind. It must have amused Owain Allington very much. He had then bought Allington Park with the proceeds. That must have amused him a great deal more. Moreover it had all happened round about the time that those ugly rumours were rendering it expedient that he should change his way of life. He had done so. He had become the model of an English landed proprietor that he now was.

It suddenly came to Appleby – but with the effect of an aside which he mustn't spend too much time on – that Allington had been playing some sort of joke on young Tristram Travis too. He had deliberately put him in the way of finding the record which he himself had already found and profited by. He had probably fostered Travis' relationship with Hope Allington. And he had been watching them scheming to possess themselves of what was no longer there in the lake. Since his scientific career had come to its dubious end, time had been hanging rather heavily on Owain Allington's hands.

But at this point the picture gave out. Owain Allington was the centre of the jigsaw puzzle. Appleby now had no doubt about that. But there was one piece missing. And it was missing – one had to say – plumb in the centre of the figure of Owain Allington himself.

Appleby knew precisely what he wanted to lay his hand on. But at the moment he was scanning the table for it in vain.

'Just here,' Colonel Pride said. 'It's getting a bit dark for a recce, but you can see the idea. A pretty sheer drop. Still, you could say he might have hit his head on something on the way down. Odd sort of place. Fake, of course. Even the little precipice.'

'I've been here before.' Appleby advanced from the base of the ruined tower, and peered down at the surface of the darkening lake. 'My wife and I walked round this way, when we'd had enough of the fête for the time being. We even asked each other what would happen if one fell over. How was the body discovered so soon?'

'A leg remained out of the water, caught in the cleft of an old shrub. He can't have been conscious, I'd say, or he would probably have got it free. Spotted by one of my men, going up the drive over there on his bicycle.'

'It's barely three hours since he was in my own house, Pride. He came to tea.'

'You don't say so!' The Chief Constable appeared to search for a relevant comment. 'Always coming to tea, aren't they?' He shook his head. 'Crazy affair, this. Three deaths. To my mind, accident won't do. What d'you think, Appleby?'

'Accident certainly won't do. Yet Scrape's end isn't self-evidently anything else. I rather think he had the habit of a potter round the lake. He started off on something of the sort with Judith and myself. This tower would be a good secluded rendezvous for a conference.'

'And for a bit of a rough house afterwards? Queer affair for a clergyman to get mixed up in. Who would want to do in this chap Scrape?' Colonel Pride shook his head in perplexity. 'Rather the crawling sort, he seemed to me. Nothing against padres in general, mark you. Salt of the earth, some of them. Remember one of them at Dunkirk. First class chap. It's the Christianity does it, I suppose.'

'I'm afraid it was Scrape's Christianity that was his undoing.'

'Good Lord!' Pride looked properly shocked. 'Bashed by the atheist, eh?'

'Not exactly that. He had rather a fanatical project in his head. He wanted to build something ecclesiastical in a big way. I'm pretty sure his death was the consequence of an injudicious fund-raising effort. He was going after the mammon of unrighteousness. It didn't work.'

'It's a comfort to me, my dear Appleby, that you appear to be getting a grip on this damned thing.' A shade of dubiety might have been detected in Pride's voice. It was evident that he felt Scrape's getting himself murdered had been something wholly improper in a beneficed clergyman. 'Had we better be getting back to the house?'

'I suppose so.' Suddenly Appleby pointed across the head of the lake. 'The end of the drive is just over there. Have you noticed whether any electricity runs down to it from the house?'

'I'm sure it doesn't. And there isn't any on the high road. I see you're thinking that the confounded turn in ought to be lit.'

'It might have made a difference, certainly.' Appleby turned round. 'The castle looks rather well against the evening sky. The house too, for that matter. Allington's rather a lovely place, really. It's a pity it should be stained by three revolting murders. And they'll be remembered – if you ask me – for rather a long time.'

'Three murders!'

'We certainly have to face up to that, Pride. And we must just hope it stops there.'

8

'A confoundedly upsetting day,' Ivon Lethbridge said. Appleby and Pride had run into him in the hall. 'Inconsiderate to the last.' He seemed to become aware of a certain incomprehension in his hearers. 'Martin behaving like that. Choosing the doorstep to die on, you might say. Of course the kids have got wind of it. They had wind of it last night, if you ask me. And then the yokel as well. And now the local padre. It's outrageous.'

'Your boys are upset?' The Chief Constable spoke with rather perfunctory sympathy. 'Too bad. Fond of their uncle, no doubt.'

'Nothing of the sort!' Lethbridge was indignant. 'Of course my wife had taught them that Martin was a precious blackguard. She's very strict. A right-thinking woman. At least since our marriage. Made her toe the line.'

A loud guffaw greeted this. It came, naturally, from the robust Charity Lethbridge, who had entered the hall.

'No laughing matter.' For once, Lethbridge was offended by his wife's levity. 'Hopelessly off their game. We kept them at it all day, you know. Only thing to do. But Digby's topspin has followed Eugene's down the drain. Desperate situation. George's kids too. Can't hole a two-foot putt, George says. Serious thing, at that formative age.' He looked round. 'Ah, here *is* George. Pack up and clear out's the word, if you ask me. George, what do you think?'

'First thing in the morning.' George Barford nodded vigorously. 'I've told Faith to get our traps together tonight. Of course the brats are all asleep now. But we had a shocking afternoon.' He turned to

Appleby. 'We caught them at some sort of make-believe. Pretending to be gangsters, or pirates, or Lord knows what. Thin end of the wedge, eh? But I'm not going to have my daughters grow up to waste their time. I'm damned if I am.'

'You are afraid,' Appleby asked, 'that these unfortunate events have stimulated the children's imaginations?'

'That's it. Deuced well put.' Barford was honest in his admiration for this degree of linguistic resource.

'And I caught Digby,' Lethbridge said, 'yarning with that young egg-head who hangs around the place. Fellow called Travis, out of some Oxford college. Wants to lay Hope, if you ask me. Sorry, m'dear.' Very properly, Lethbridge apologized to his wife for this crude expression – and received a blast of hilarity in exchange. 'Talking to the kid about treasure-hunting, or some such rot. Know this Travis, Sir John?'

'I've had a little conversation with him. There is something to be said for the view that he is a rather frivolous and irresponsible young man. Or that he turns into that, when he knows that he has to call it a day. Your sister Hope is plainly a different type. But they might suit each other very well. And now, if you will excuse us, I think the Chief Constable and I must seek out Mr Allington.'

'He's in the library,' Barford said, 'with your wife and that old fellow Osborne. Deuced lot of people crowding in on this affair.'

'Well, well!' Pride murmured, as he and Appleby walked away. 'Straightforward chaps, and all that. But just a little…wouldn't you say? All right among city types, no doubt. But wouldn't go down too well in a decent regiment.'

Appleby received this grim condemnation in appropriate silence. He had no reason to doubt that it wasn't entirely true.

The curtains had been drawn in the library. Here and there a low reading lamp had been turned on, so that the room existed only as so many pools of light fading into shadow. This made it look larger than it really was. Appleby hadn't entered it since the occasion described by Owain Allington as a congenial *tête-à-tête*. But that had been only forty-eight hours ago. The mysterious affair at Allington Park, he told himself grimly, was going to be wound up, like a reasonably regular tragedy, in just a little over two revolutions of the sun.

There were thousands of books in imposing rows, with marble busts of Homer, Dante, Shakespeare, and similar appropriate persons perched above them near the ceiling. Presumably the first Mr Osborne had given orders for the bringing together of such approved authors as an English gentleman must be able to put his hand upon at need – and there they all were, from the Elizabethan translations of Philemon Holland to the sermons of Bishop Beilby Porteus. And subsequent Osbornes had added further essential works which Appleby could guess at without looking: the Badminton Library, Burton's *Arabian Nights*, Egan's *Boxiana*, bound volumes of *Vanity Fair* and *Cornhill* and *Punch*, romances by Edgar Wallace, bulky memoirs with titles like *Our Viceregal Life in India*. Owain Allington had presumably taken over the lot. What his own taste in reading would be, Appleby didn't know.

The room was precisely as it had been two nights before. Rasselas was in his familiar posture on the black rug. He might have been a pneumatic dog, Appleby thought, able partially to deflate himself when in repose. Or he had the appearance of some low but gorgeous form of marine life, organized mainly in thread-like tentacles, floating in profound unconsciousness on a midnight sea. Rasselas had certainly withdrawn from the mysterious affair – supposing, indeed, that he could ever be credited with having had any involvement in it.

'My dear Appleby, your wife has been doing me a great kindness.' Allington had advanced, hospitably carrying a decanter. 'She has quieted my three excellent but excitable Italian women. They live out, you know – two at the farm and the third with the water-bailiff's wife – and they were reluctant even to be conducted back by Enzo. This third accident has alarmed them very much. Not that there have been *three* accidents, as you and I know.'

Appleby accepted whisky. Pride did the same, and then thought better of it. The thought had no doubt come to him that he was a police officer on duty. Judith was politely drinking what looked like ginger ale. Wilfred Osborne sat quietly in a corner, with folded arms. He looked unhappy. He had been born in this house, after all, and its park and lake had been his playground as a boy. He was taking a little hard what was so rapidly becoming its murderous character.

'I concur in your view that we are not confronting three accidents,' Appleby said to Allington. 'But I'm not very sure that our agreement will stretch much further. May I ask how you class Scrape's death?'

'It's fairly clear, isn't it?' Allington set down the decanter, and raised his own whisky-glass as if for appraisal. 'The poor fellow made away with himself. Two deaths, one on top of the other, were too much for him. He was an unbalanced man. Indeed – and this is something I've never mentioned to anybody before – I was coming to a strong suspicion that he was no longer in his right mind. You'll hardly believe this, but he had a fantastic notion of building a complete Cistercian abbey. Only – so far as I could gather – without any Cistercians.'

'Yes, I know about that.'

'You know about it!' Allington seemed really startled.

'My wife and I were entertaining Scrape to tea within what was to prove a couple of hours of his death. He mentioned his plans.'

'Then there you are.' Allington spoke incisively. 'You agree – you both agree – that he was off his head?'

'In a limited sense, yes. It doesn't follow that he made away with himself. May I ask whether you still hold to the view that your nephew met his death as the consequence of some sort of international conspiracy?'

'No, I don't.' Allington paused, perhaps to note that Appleby was startled in his turn. 'I have found myself obliged to re-think the whole thing.'

'Meaning your nephew's death and Knockdown's?'

'Precisely so. And Scrape's, indeed, in the sense that I have had to get it clear that his unfortunate end has been purely peripheral. Perhaps I can put it best by saying that I have approached the problem as a scientist. I have no doubt – Pride, you will support me in this – that the police nowadays pursue what they would call scientific methods.'

'They *are* scientific methods.' Pride was suddenly roused to something like anger. 'Not much my sort of thing, I'll admit. But I have a thoroughly up-to-date crowd. Complete confidence in them.'

'My dear man, you mustn't mistake me. I have no doubt that your men will apply their techniques with diligence, and eventually be in a position to declare that they have arrived at an explanation. And the same holds of Appleby, whom we all so much admire. Only I doubt whether, in this particular case, they will really get quite all the way. The method is one thing. The mind behind it is another. And I may say I have had to think quite hard about the problem myself.'

'To arrive at the true and final solution?' It was with some natural astonishment that Appleby had received the sudden flash of arrogance in Allington's speech. 'Do I understand that, as a consequence of powerful cerebration, you have arrived at the truth about these obscure events?'

'Certainly. I am saying just that.'

'And that your view now is that the final score – or the score to date – is two accidents and a suicide?'

'My dear Sir John' – Allington spoke with a sudden urbane courtesy – 'you will forgive me if I say that I do not judge it necessary to discuss the matter with you further.'

'Very well.' Appleby put down his glass. Judith and Osborne were already on their feet. 'You are perfectly in order, and I do not disapprove of what you say in any way. We will leave you with the Chief Constable at once, and you can tell him what you know.'

'I have no intention of telling Pride anything.'

There was a moment's blank silence – in which Rasselas, most unexpectedly, emitted the faintest of contented sighs. The creature had been visited, perhaps, by a pleasing dream. Wilfred Osborne was the first to speak.

'I say, Allington – isn't this getting a bit off the rails? Here is your own nephew come to an unhappy end, and you saying you have got to the truth of the affair. As good as saying, for that matter, that you are the only person who *will* get to the truth of the affair. You can't withhold your information from the police.'

'I am not withholding information. I am withholding speculation and inference. Call them scientific speculation and inference. I am certainly not obliged to communicate these to anybody.'

'But be reasonable, my dear Allington! What justification can you have for holding back what may be helpful? We're not all engaged in a competition, or a battle of wits.'

'I don't want to offend you, Osborne. I am beholden to you in a number of ways.' Allington was suddenly presenting the appearance of a man in real distress of mind. 'And I know you have a high sense of duties of hospitality. Well, I will say only this. I am deeply sorry that I have implicated somebody – somebody whom I am not prepared to name – in this luckless and tragic business. I decline to be an occasion of further distress – to that person, and to others. And I therefore intend that this whole business stop here. Martin had an accident with his car. The inquisitive Knockdown meddled with something carelessly left lethal, and paid for it. The unfortunate Scrape, overwrought by these fatalities, drowned himself. This may not be what I believe. It is what I have declined to discuss. And it is as much as all the Queen's coroners, and all her policemen too, are ever likely to arrive at.'

This time, the silence in the library prolonged itself. Not even Rasselas relieved it with another faint woof. And then – faintly at first but in rapidly mounting crescendo – pandemonium appeared to break out in Allington Park. It had nothing to do with the bizarre attitude and utterance of the owner of the mansion. It appeared to break out first on a bedroom floor, and then to come tumbling rapidly down the main staircase.

A moment later, the library seemed suddenly filled with Lethbridges and Barfords. But in fact it was only the parents who had come tumbling in.

'The kids!' Ivon Lethbridge shouted. 'All four of them. They've vanished. They've been carried off. Without so much as climbing into their beds!'

'Murder!' The sudden scream came from Faith Barford. 'Murder, murder, *murder!*'

9

For some moments the distressing character of this scene was enhanced by Hope Allington, who had come briskly into the drawing-room and at once addressed herself to smacking her sister's face. Although a time-sanctioned treatment for hysterical behaviour, it lacked amenity as a family spectacle. But at least it had some effect. Faith Barford stopped screaming and subsided into quiet sobs.

She was not altogether to be blamed, Appleby thought. The atmosphere at Allington Park was now such that any untoward event was likely to be accorded a sinister interpretation. In any well-regulated English mind three unaccountable deaths add up to the probable presence of a maniac about the place. Within such a context the sudden disappearance of four children might well disturb anyone.

'Miss Allington,' Appleby asked, 'where is Mr Travis now?'

'Back in Oxford.' Hope snapped this out frankly enough. 'We decided that it was no go. Either way – whether it's still there or not – there's nothing in it for us.'

'My dear Hope,' Owain Allington said, 'whatever are you talking about? This is no time to speak in riddles.'

'Isn't that just what you've been doing yourself?' Appleby said. 'And I don't think there's much of a riddle in what Miss Allington tells us, anyway. But we'd better get back to the children. I think, Miss Allington, that Mr Travis had some talk with them?'

'Oh, yes. He told them the story of the siege. Good Cavalier and Roundhead stuff. They loved it. Tristram said afterwards that he thought he could make historians of Eugene and Digby.'

'Historians!' The natural agitation of Ivon Lethbridge modulated into indignation before this. 'Cavaliers and Roundheads? Damned nonsense! History is all bunk, as Winston Churchill said.'

'I think that Mr Lethbridge is perhaps confusing his authorities,' Appleby suggested mildly. 'But again we must stick to the point. The children had better be found at once. But there is probably very little mystery about them. Miss Allington, may I take it that Mr Travis amused himself by telling them the wonderful story of the treasure as well?'

'It's quite likely – and why shouldn't he?'

'Why indeed? But here are two high-spirited boys bored stiff by top-spin' – Appleby had to hold up a hand to check the just indignation of the Lethbridge parents before this appalling remark – 'and along with them two admiring girl-cousins. I have very little doubt that they're having a wonderful time in the castle at this moment. If not there, then somewhere else around the place. I suggest that some of us go and see.'

'It's pitch dark by now,' Judith said. 'And there will be no moon for hours.'

'We'll want as many electric torches as can be found.' Appleby said. 'We'll also want a certain discretion. There's no need to alarm them with the effect of a hue and cry.' He turned to Allington. 'And do you think we might venture to disturb Rasselas? He might be quite a help.'

'You're right about not alarming them,' Wilfred Osborne murmured to Appleby as the expedition set out. 'If I had children as young as these at Allington, I'd put the castle out of bounds.'

'The ruins are dangerous?'

'I think they must be called that. There are one or two places with an ugly drop to the moat. And one or two others where masonry might come tumbling during a scramble.'

'I see. It's something the clever Mr Travis might have thought of before putting ideas in the children's heads. Judith was wrong about its being pitch dark. It's a perfectly clear sky, and starlight counts for something, when one's eyes get used to it. Still, the children are almost sure to have torches themselves, and that should help. Just catch a glimpse of one of them, and we can begin making friendly and unalarming noises.'

'John, is that you?' Judith's voice came out of the darkness, and in a moment she had joined them. 'Aren't we rather a crowd?'

'Yes, we are. But one could hardly expect anyone to stay behind.' Appleby glanced at the straggle of torches around them. 'Ten of us, I think. It's a bit intimidating. Do you think we should split up?'

'I think the castle can be left to the others. Tommy Pride will keep them in order. This is just his sort of thing.'

'Yes – not quite what he calls a recce, but an operation of a related sort.' Appleby suddenly made up his mind. 'We three will go down the drive. Wilfred, do you agree?'

'Certainly, my dear John. I was going to suggest it, as a matter of fact. If the children know where their uncle Martin was drowned –'

'I have an idea there isn't much they don't know.'

'Quite so. Well, the end of the lake may, at the moment, have a morbid fascination for them.'

'A romantic fascination as well,' Judith said. 'If young Mr Travis spun them a yarn about the treasure, he may have told them that it is at the bottom of the lake, somewhere near the bridge. If he has checked out as a treasure-hunter himself, it might amuse him to turn Eugene, Digby, Sandra, and Stephanie on to the job. He wouldn't see anything irresponsible in it.'

'Come on, then.' Appleby had turned in his tracks. 'I'd rather like a fourth in the person of Rasselas. But I think he's leading the cavalcade to the castle.'

'Yes,' Judith said – and murmured, 'Here's a fourth, all the same.'

It was Owain Allington, who had caught up with them unseen. He flashed his torch briefly by way of identifying them.

'A change of plan?' he asked.

'We're going down the drive,' Appleby said. 'The one by the lake. As far as the road and the bridge. We think it's possible they may be down there.'

'I can't think why. But I'll come with you, all the same. Not that I feel this commotion is necessary. There are no criminals lurking round Allington – '

'It wasn't your former view,' Appleby said.

'Never mind my former view. These children are certainly out on a prank, as you have said. No harm is likely to befall them.'

'Osborne says that the castle is rather dangerous ground. And I'm not sure the same isn't to be said of the deeper part of the lake.'

'That is true.' Owain Allington's voice sounded indifferent in the darkness. 'But Eugene and Digby are perfectly sensible boys. They are even intelligent boys – which is surprising, when you consider their imbecile parents.' The voice was now contemptuous. 'They won't run the little girls into anything foolish. Or not intentionally. Of course, one can't insure against sheer chance. It *is* possible to set someone to a fatal prank – without knowing what one is about.'

Silence succeeded upon this odd remark of Allington's. They were now on the drive, and making good speed towards the high road. Glancing back over his left shoulder, Appleby could see the flickering and waving torches of the other party now approaching the castle – which itself showed in barely perceptible silhouette against the night sky. Appleby halted, and turned to look directly back up the drive. The form of the house too ought to have been visible, but was obscured behind the curved line of lights on the terrace. He told himself that he was looking straight at the heart of at least Martin Allington's mystery. But he had known this for some time. Unfortunately the knowledge was of no use to him. It would remain of no use to him until one final piece of the jigsaw puzzle turned up and was fitted into place.

'I think I hear something,' Wilfred Osborne said.

'And I think they've got a camp-fire.' Judith had come to a standstill. 'It seems almost a shame to break in on them.' She laughed softly. 'John, our own children used to do just this sort of thing.'

'And your grandchildren,' Osborne said, 'will be doing it in no time.' He put a hand on Judith's arm. 'And the grandparents will be more alarmed than the parents are.' He paused comfortably on this bachelor's wisdom. 'Allington, don't you agree?'

'I know no more about parenthood than you do.' It was with a sudden harshness that Owain Allington's voice came out of the darkness. 'But these children are up to some devilry which must be stopped.'

'Yes,' Appleby said. 'I'm against devilry. And it's not all devilry that gets stopped in time.'

It was a very jolly little camp-fire. Among its materials Appleby could discern several of those hurdles which the detective police are fond of carrying around for the purpose of screening the sites of mysterious or unseemly occurrences from the public view. On either side of it sat one of the Misses Barford. Sandra was in a nightdress and jodhpurs. Stephanie was wearing a cricket-shirt and a pair of shorts so much too big for her that they must certainly have been borrowed from one of her cousins for the occasion. Digby was standing by the edge of the lake. Unlike the companions of the reprehensible Richard Cyphus on the previous day, he was decorously clad in a bathing-slip. He was also clad in an unbelievable amount of mud. From the lake itself came splashing and gasping sounds. Then out of it emerged first the dripping head of Eugene, and then Eugene's right arm, raised triumphantly aloft. He was grasping what appeared to be an old boot, and with this he scrambled up the bank and tumbled panting on the grass. He too was wearing a bathing-slip, and he too was coated in mud. But one day, Appleby saw, he was going to be a beautifully proportioned youth. The prison-house of Wimbledon, in fact, lay ineluctably in front of him. He would vault the net to shake hands with his defeated foe. He would duck his head at royalty as he left the Centre court. He would make awkward and modest remarks to television interviewers thereafter. But at the moment he was a boy, and diving for treasure.

'Hullo,' Appleby said cheerfully. 'Found anything much as yet?'

'Everything's over here.' It was Digby who replied, since Eugene lacked the breath with which to do so. Perhaps in the absence of his robust parents, Digby was quietly polite and wholly composed. 'It's not much so far, but we think it rather hopeful.'

The treasure-trove to date was ranged neatly on a bathing-towel. There was a dead fish. There was a horseshoe – which Digby picked up and exhibited with gravity, remarking that it might do quite well second-hand. There were several other iron objects of indeterminate shape. Eugene, coming up a little apprehensively, was of the opinion that these had undoubtedly formed part of the treasure-chest itself. There were some bottles, which seemed extremely old, and might therefore be sold to a museum. There was a whistle, which unfortunately didn't look as if it could antedate the police force or the Boy Scout movement, and into which Digby blew vigorously but with an inaudible result. There was a single coin which Sandra was cleaning vigorously. When it was handed to Appleby, he was a good deal impressed to find that it was an Elizabethan shilling-piece.

'That's certainly a find,' he said. 'Really enough for one night, don't you think? And deep-sea divers never work more than rather short spells. And here's Rasselas come to take you back to the house.'

It was true that Rasselas had arrived. The normally stately creature, indeed, had come racing down the drive at high speed. Presumably he had deserted the Chief Constable and his band – whose torches could now be clearly seen, moving about among the castle ruins.

'We'd better let them know that all's well,' Wilfred Osborne suggested. 'I'll walk over at once.'

'A good idea,' Appleby said. 'And perhaps Judith will go back to the house with the explorers and Rasselas. More treasure-hunting tomorrow, perhaps. I'd like to see Eugene and Digby diving. They must be better than some older boys I know. Allington and I will perhaps just have a final look round.'

These dispositions were put in train at once – the more readily because the children, who had no doubt felt certain misgivings upon the irruption of the grown-up world, had been treated as rational beings, and were disposed to behave rationally as a result. Appleby and Allington, left alone in the darkness, were both silent for a few moments.

'We'll take the night's catch up to the house with us,' Appleby said presently. 'It has its interest.'

'I hardly think we need take the fish. But the Elizabethan coin is curious, I agree.'

'One would expect a few scattered coins to be left down there on the bed of the lake. But to retrieve one like that was a remarkable feat. I really do think rather well of those boys.' Appleby was silent again, gazing up the drive at the lighted terrace in the distance. 'It's so simple,' he said quietly. 'So absolutely simple. Once you see it. Twelve o'clock and two o'clock.'

'I'm afraid I don't follow you.'

'It's how we used to be taught to locate objects. Don't you remember? In the OTC, for instance. Straight up there is the house, and we'll call it twelve o'clock. So the castle – where they're still fooling around with their torches, you notice – is as near two o'clock as makes no difference. Slantwise across the lake.'

'I take it, Appleby, you're claiming to know just what happened on the night Martin died?'

'Yes – and I'm only following in your footsteps. You've been making the same claim yourself. And announcing that you're going to keep mum about it. Well, I'm afraid the truth is going to be made known.'

'It must be?'

'Of course it must.'

'I am so sorry. I really do regret it very much. I feel terribly to blame.' As he made these strange remarks, Allington produced a cigarette-case, opened it, and extended it to Appleby. 'Won't you smoke?' he said. 'It will keep the midges away. And it's a mild night. We might talk this out quietly – don't you think? – before returning to the house.'

'Very well,' Appleby said, and took a cigarette. 'We'll talk it out.'

Gate One glimmered on its bank. Appleby walked over and sat down on it. He could, he felt, afford to relax. The entire mysterious affair was now elucidated. Nothing further of an unexpected sort could happen.

'You killed my nephew,' Owain Allington said.

10

There was a moment's blank silence. The night was very still – as still as the night had been when Appleby had sat in Allington's library, constrained by an excessive hospitality to stop rather longer than he had wanted to. No owls. No frogs. Not a sound.

'Did I kill Knockdown and Scrape as well?' Appleby asked. He was wondering whether the madman standing in front of him carried a concealed weapon. Short of that, he could tackle him easily enough.

'Of course not. Knockdown's death was a matter of sheer misadventure befalling an intruder. We have established that. Poor Scrape was thrown off his balance by what had happened, and by his exciting afternoon, and by the extravagant notions that had been gaining on him. He simply drowned himself – hitting his head on something as he went down.'

'So I killed only Martin Allington. It wasn't your first idea, I'd remind you again. There was that business about spies and international conspiracy. Perhaps that was just to protect me?'

'Of course. I was determined not to embarrass a guest.'

'I see.' Appleby took a long breath. 'Even although he was a murderer?'

'You know very well that there is no question of murder. I simply implicated you in a fatal prank. Not even that, indeed. It wasn't unreasonable that I should show you the *son et lumière*. It was idle – nothing more than idle – to invite you to have a go.'

'I remember the words,' Appleby said.

'Well, you understand what happened. I knew that you understood what happened, as soon as you said that about twelve o'clock and two o'clock.' Allington turned and pointed. 'Swing into this drive in the dark, and you expect to see the lights on the terrace straight ahead of you. Twelve o'clock. Anybody accustomed to arrive by night would have that expectation. But suppose those lights had just gone out, and an almost identical line of lights had sprung up before the castle. Two o'clock. Instinctively, and for a fatal fraction of time, you would steer for that. And it's what took poor Martin into the lake. Appleby, I repeat that I really do regret it very much. I hate your having the consciousness of such a thing on your hands – utterly innocent though it was.'

'I'm very much obliged to you.' Appleby's tone was grim. 'I certainly flicked a switch – and the effect was to send the lights on the terrace leap-frogging over the lake and in front of the castle. Would you care to offer any estimate of the length of time they stayed like that?'

'Oh, quite some time.'

'I think not. In no time we had the effect of the castle burning. No one would steer a car at *that*.'

'It is scarcely material. The coincidence was a dreadful one, in any case. It may have been in the split second that you flicked that switch that Martin swung into the drive.'

'It was nothing of the sort.' Appleby got to his feet. During the next few minutes, he judged, he might be safer that way. 'It was between fifteen and twenty minutes earlier.'

'You have a freakish streak to you,' Appleby said, 'as well as an alarmingly criminal one. You are also a bit of a showman, as you blandly told me yourself. As a practical physicist, of course, you are superannuated. But – and you told me this too – you still get a great deal of fun out of quite small projects. You called the *son et lumière* "all that rot" – but added that you took an active part in rigging it up. The words are fair enough.'

'I'm not sure,' Allington said, 'that this discussion, my dear Appleby, isn't taking an injudicious turn.'

'Perhaps it is. But I don't recommend too abrupt an end to it.' Appleby had observed in Allington a disposition to let his right hand hover over a pocket. 'You can't accidentally drown *me*, you know. And anything else wouldn't be of much use to you. May I go on?'

'Go on.'

'You were being steadily blackmailed by your disagreeable nephew. He knew something quite fatal about that scandal you believed you had escaped so successfully. He forced you to make him your heir. I rather think he knew about the treasure, and had extorted his share of that too. It is no doubt the reason why you decided he was to perish where he did – dead on the site of it. The difficulty you faced was that there is no electricity down at this end of the drive. Running a system of hidden wires so far would have been much too risky. But up at the house and castle the situation was quite different. Amid all the litter of the *son et lumière*, you could do pretty well anything you pleased – and clear away all trace of it again in an hour or so. I don't know how you made the acquaintance of Knockdown.'

'Knockdown? What an abrupt transition! Knockdown comes into this fantasy?'

'You were acquainted with Knockdown. And poor Scrape – unfortunately for him – knew you were. But, for the moment, that is by the way. You enrolled Knockdown as an accomplice, and the rest was perfectly easy. Even sending him to his own death was perfectly easy. When he had, in fact, served your turn, he had your instructions – he was a biddable man, remember, and of low intelligence – to make his way to the gazebo and operate some switch concealed under a bench. It killed him. And you, who were the first to climb up to the place, had only to give him a small shove in order to render him unnoticeable. It was only when you had put me through the business of accidentally killing your nephew – who was, of course, dead already – that you drew attention to him. He had died instantly, and could never give evidence against you.'

There was a long silence. Here and there, the dark surface of the lake threw up the reflection of a star. Beyond, there was a flickering of torchlight as the party which had been searching the castle began to return to the house. Wilfred Osborne must have reached them with the news that all was well.

'Rasselas,' Appleby said, 'is a very well-trained dog.'

Again there was silence. It was followed by a gulping sound, which for a moment Appleby supposed to come from the man standing motionless before him. Then he realized that it came from the lake. Disturbed by Eugene and Digby Lethbridge, the muddy depth was sending up an occasional gassy bubble to explode in air.

'Timing was the key to the matter,' Appleby said. 'I was conscious, in a vague way, of time as behaving queerly. I was being manipulated through it with some very nice calculation. I wasn't alone in that.'

'Did you say something about Rasselas?' Allington asked.

'Yes.' Appleby bent down to Eugene and Digby's small hoard. 'Here's the key. Only it isn't a key. It's a whistle.'

'I see the whistle.' Allington appeared to examine the small object closely. 'Just a whistle.'

'The obedient Knockdown, following instructions, threw it into the lake as soon as he'd used it. And then – it was a chance in a thousand – the boys brought it out.'

'Just why did Knockdown use a whistle?'

'It was his signal to you that Martin's car was approaching.'

'My dear man, you're crazy. According to your account, we were together in the library as Martin was approaching the drive. We certainly heard no whistle – and nothing else either.'

'I agree. But Rasselas did. It's that sort of whistle. You saw Digby blow it a few minutes ago, and we hardly heard a sound. But Rasselas heard it – from as far away as the castle. And he was here in no time.'

'It was Rasselas who killed my nephew?'

'That sort of whistle is a man-made equivalent of the squeak of a bat. The pitch is too high to be audible at least to adult human ears, but a dog will hear it, and can be trained to respond to it at once.

Nowadays, one sees people using such things regularly in public parks. By the way, you couldn't stop yourself from looking expectantly at Rasselas from time to time. And then the moment came. Knockdown gave the signal. Rasselas rose and went straight to the door. You pressed a bell – for Enzo, who was no longer in the house. Only it was no longer a bell. It switched off the lights on the terrace, and switched on the lights at the castle. Then, in perhaps five or six minutes, it reversed the process. Easy for you to rig. Easy for you to destroy all traces of – perhaps next morning, perhaps that night. Knockdown was dead – but no policeman was going to cast a vigilant eye on you because of that. By the time Martin's death was discovered, even the last traces of the *son et lumière* had vanished. Scrape was the only unexpected complication. And simply because he knew you had lied about Knockdown. He thought things out. But you weren't going to be blackmailed a second time – not even in the interest of a Cistercian abbey. So you suggested a quiet talk while walking round the lake. Incidentally, you have suggested *this* quiet talk with me. But, as I've said, it won't do. You can't drown me. You can only shoot. Well, shoot away – and face Pride's men afterwards.'

'Might we perhaps move back to the house?' Owain Allington had turned away. 'The others may be wondering what has happened to us.'

'Yes, we'll go back.'

'Perhaps, my dear Appleby, I might stroll ahead. You may want to take a final look round so interesting a spot.'

It was a strange moment – and then Appleby told himself that he was no longer a policeman.

'Yes, of course,' he said.

He sat down again on Gate One, and gazed fixedly at the lake. It was a full two minutes before he heard the shot. He rose and walked slowly towards it. The mysterious affair was over.

MICHAEL INNES

APPLEBY ON ARARAT

Inspector Appleby is stranded on a very strange island, with a rather odd bunch of people – too many men, too few women (and one of them too attractive) cause a deal of trouble. But that is nothing compared to later developments, including the body afloat in the water and the attack by local inhabitants.

'Every sentence he writes has flavour, every incident flamboyance'
– *Times Literary Supplement*

THE DAFFODIL AFFAIR

Inspector Appleby's aunt is most distressed when her horse, Daffodil – a somewhat half-witted animal with exceptional numerical skills – goes missing from her stable in Harrogate. Meanwhile, Hudspith is hot on the trail of Lucy Rideout, an enigmatic young girl who has been whisked away to an unknown isle by a mysterious gentleman. And when a house in Bloomsbury, supposedly haunted, also goes missing, the baffled policemen search for a connection. As Appleby and Hudspith trace Daffodil and Lucy, the fragments begin to come together and an extravagant project is uncovered, leading them to a South American jungle.

'Yet another surprising firework display of wit and erudition and ingenious invention' – *Guardian*

MICHAEL INNES

DEATH AT THE PRESIDENT'S LODGING

Inspector Appleby is called to St Anthony's College, where the President has been murdered in his Lodging. Scandal abounds when it becomes clear that the only people with any motive to murder him are the only people who had the opportunity – because the President's Lodging opens off Orchard Ground, which is locked at night, and only the Fellows of the College have keys…

'It is quite the most accomplished first crime novel that I have read…all first-rate entertainment'
– Cecil Day Lewis, *The Daily Telegraph*

HAMLET, REVENGE!

At Seamnum Court, seat of the Duke of Horton, The Lord Chancellor of England is murdered at the climax of a private presentation of *Hamlet*, in which he plays Polonius. Inspector Appleby pursues some of the most famous names in the country, unearthing dreadful suspicion.

'Michael Innes is in a class by himself among writers of detective fiction' – *Times Literary Supplement*

MICHAEL INNES

THE LONG FAREWELL

Lewis Packford, the great Shakespearean scholar, was thought to have discovered a book annotated by the Bard – but there is no trace of this valuable object when Packford apparently commits suicide. Sir John Appleby finds a mixed bag of suspects at the dead man's house, who might all have a good motive for murder. The scholars and bibliophiles who were present might have been tempted by the precious document in Packford's possession. And Appleby discovers that Packford had two secret marriages, and that both of these women were at the house at the time of his death.

A PRIVATE VIEW

Sir John and Lady Appleby attend a memorial exhibition of the oils, gouaches, collages and *trouvailles* of artist Gavin Limbert, who was recently found shot under very suspicious circumstances. As Assistant-Commissioner of Police, Sir John is already interested, but he becomes even more intrigued when Limbert's last masterpiece is stolen from the gallery under his very eyes.

'Exciting, amusingly written…very good enjoyment it is'
– *The Spectator*

TITLES BY MICHAEL INNES AVAILABLE DIRECT
FROM HOUSE OF STRATUS

Quantity		£	$(US)	$(CAN)	€
	THE AMPERSAND PAPERS	6.99	12.95	19.95	13.50
	APPLEBY AND HONEYBATH	6.99	12.95	19.95	13.50
	APPLEBY AND THE OSPREYS	6.99	12.95	19.95	13.50
	THE APPLEBY FILE	6.99	12.95	19.95	13.50
	APPLEBY ON ARARAT	6.99	12.95	19.95	13.50
	APPLEBY PLAYS CHICKEN	6.99	12.95	19.95	13.50
	APPLEBY TALKING	6.99	12.95	19.95	13.50
	APPLEBY TALKS AGAIN	6.99	12.95	19.95	13.50
	APPLEBY'S ANSWER	6.99	12.95	19.95	13.50
	APPLEBY'S END	6.99	12.95	19.95	13.50
	APPLEBY'S OTHER STORY	6.99	12.95	19.95	13.50
	AN AWKWARD LIE	6.99	12.95	19.95	13.50
	THE BLOODY WOOD	6.99	12.95	19.95	13.50
	CARSON'S CONSPIRACY	6.99	12.95	19.95	13.50
	A CHANGE OF HEIR	6.99	12.95	19.95	13.50
	CHRISTMAS AT CANDLESHOE	6.99	12.95	19.95	13.50
	A CONNOISSEUR'S CASE	6.99	12.95	19.95	13.50
	THE DAFFODIL AFFAIR	6.99	12.95	19.95	13.50
	DEATH AT THE CHASE	6.99	12.95	19.95	13.50
	DEATH AT THE PRESIDENT'S LODGING	6.99	12.95	19.95	13.50
	A FAMILY AFFAIR	6.99	12.95	19.95	13.50
	FROM LONDON FAR	6.99	12.95	19.95	13.50
	THE GAY PHOENIX	6.99	12.95	19.95	13.50
	GOING IT ALONE	6.99	12.95	19.95	13.50

ALL HOUSE OF STRATUS BOOKS ARE AVAILABLE FROM GOOD BOOKSHOPS
OR DIRECT FROM THE PUBLISHER:

Internet: **www.houseofstratus.com** including synopses and features.

Email: **sales@houseofstratus.com**
info@houseofstratus.com
(please quote author, title and credit card details.)

TITLES BY MICHAEL INNES AVAILABLE DIRECT
FROM HOUSE OF STRATUS

Quantity		£	$(US)	$(CAN)	€
	HAMLET, REVENGE!	6.99	12.95	19.95	13.50
	HARE SITTING UP	6.99	12.95	19.95	13.50
	HONEYBATH'S HAVEN	6.99	12.95	19.95	13.50
	THE JOURNEYING BOY	6.99	12.95	19.95	13.50
	LAMENT FOR A MAKER	6.99	12.95	19.95	13.50
	THE LONG FAREWELL	6.99	12.95	19.95	13.50
	LORD MULLION'S SECRET	6.99	12.95	19.95	13.50
	THE MAN FROM THE SEA	6.99	12.95	19.95	13.50
	MONEY FROM HOLME	6.99	12.95	19.95	13.50
	THE MYSTERIOUS COMMISSION	6.99	12.95	19.95	13.50
	THE NEW SONIA WAYWARD	6.99	12.95	19.95	13.50
	A NIGHT OF ERRORS	6.99	12.95	19.95	13.50
	OLD HALL, NEW HALL	6.99	12.95	19.95	13.50
	THE OPEN HOUSE	6.99	12.95	19.95	13.50
	OPERATION PAX	6.99	12.95	19.95	13.50
	A PRIVATE VIEW	6.99	12.95	19.95	13.50
	THE SECRET VANGUARD	6.99	12.95	19.95	13.50
	SHEIKS AND ADDERS	6.99	12.95	19.95	13.50
	SILENCE OBSERVED	6.99	12.95	19.95	13.50
	STOP PRESS	6.99	12.95	19.95	13.50
	THERE CAME BOTH MIST AND SNOW	6.99	12.95	19.95	13.50
	THE WEIGHT OF THE EVIDENCE	6.99	12.95	19.95	13.50
	WHAT HAPPENED AT HAZELWOOD	6.99	12.95	19.95	13.50

ALL HOUSE OF STRATUS BOOKS ARE AVAILABLE FROM GOOD BOOKSHOPS
OR DIRECT FROM THE PUBLISHER:

Tel:	**Order Line**
	0800 169 1780 (UK)
	International
	+44 (0) 1845 527700 (UK)
Fax:	**+44 (0) 1845 527711 (UK)**
	(please quote author, title and credit card details.)
Send to:	**House of Stratus Sales Department**
	Thirsk Industrial Park
	York Road, Thirsk
	North Yorkshire, YO7 3BX
	UK

PAYMENT

Please tick currency you wish to use:

☐ £ (Sterling)   ☐ $ (US)   ☐ $ (CAN)   ☐ € (Euros)

Allow for shipping costs charged per order plus an amount per book as set out in the tables below:

CURRENCY/DESTINATION

	£(Sterling)	$(US)	$(CAN)	€(Euros)
Cost per order				
UK	1.50	2.25	3.50	2.50
Europe	3.00	4.50	6.75	5.00
North America	3.00	3.50	5.25	5.00
Rest of World	3.00	4.50	6.75	5.00
Additional cost per book				
UK	0.50	0.75	1.15	0.85
Europe	1.00	1.50	2.25	1.70
North America	1.00	1.00	1.50	1.70
Rest of World	1.50	2.25	3.50	3.00

PLEASE SEND CHEQUE OR INTERNATIONAL MONEY ORDER
payable to: HOUSE OF STRATUS LTD or card payment as indicated

STERLING EXAMPLE

Cost of book(s):..................... Example: 3 x books at £6.99 each: £20.97
Cost of order:...................... Example: £1.50 (Delivery to UK address)
Additional cost per book:.............. Example: 3 x £0.50: £1.50
Order total including shipping:.......... Example: £23.97

VISA, MASTERCARD, SWITCH, AMEX:

☐☐☐☐☐☐☐☐☐☐☐☐☐☐☐☐☐☐☐☐

Issue number (Switch only):

☐☐☐

Start Date: Expiry Date:

☐☐/☐☐   ☐☐/☐☐

Signature: _____

NAME: _____

ADDRESS: _____

COUNTRY: _____

ZIP/POSTCODE: _____

Please allow 28 days for delivery. Despatch normally within 48 hours.

Prices subject to change without notice.
Please tick box if you do not wish to receive any additional information. ☐

House of Stratus publishes many other titles in this genre; please check our website (**www.houseofstratus.com**) for more details.